The Trail of the Fox

Mark W. Laughlin

Contents

To Riley,
my Princess.

- P

The Trail of the Fox

I

I The Trail of the Fox

Footprints

The clouds crept silently up the valley. Today they were not high in the sky, they were low, scraping their bellies on the floor of the valley as they went. Higher up, it was clear. As soon as the sun was up, these low clouds would disappear, and the hot dryness of the summer would return. Ach could see smoke at the far end of the valley, where the neighboring clan lived.

Seeing smoke was good. It meant there was no fear of raiders in the valley. Raiders come in strength, and nothing good comes with them. When strangers have been spotted, the people build low fires in their lodges at night, so the smoke is unseen in the dark. Then during the day, the women and children do their work in hidden places, no fires, no smoke, no loud talk. But the raiders had not been around for some time, and so the neighbors, and Ach's own tribe, slept without fear. They worked out in the open during the day, enjoying the warm sun of the morning, and ranging far to gather berries and other food.

Life was hard enough, digging roots, drying meat, using the warm time to prepare for the cold time. There was danger enough from animals, and sickness, and hunger. No need to add raiders to that mix. Life was much better without them.

Ach belonged to the "Rock People", named for the high rock wall that stood just behind their village. On these rocks, the sun's rays could first be seen in the morning, as they slowly crept down to the valley floor, to warm the lodge of Ach's father. The people at the high end of the valley were called the "Cloud People", for the way the clouds came up to them. The two villages had given these names to each other, names of respect, many summers ago.

Ach sat high on the ridge that divides the valley and serves as a polite, but meaningful boundary between the two neighboring tribes. It was not a line that "must not be crossed". Much to the contrary, Ach's family group was welcome there and often visited the Cloud people and traded with them. But still, it was a boundary. One should be back on his own side by nightfall, and should not be near the village of the others uninvited, and especially, nowhere near their women and children.

The other village observed the same boundary, which had been worked out long, long ago, in the time of the "Old Man's" grandfathers. A boundary like this was good. It helped maintain a respectful peace between them. As well, with the two tribes allied, which had also been for some time, other tribes had not bothered them, because together, the tribes had the strength of two.

Ach's father and the brother of his father also had the strength of two. They hunted together, their women helped each other. When trouble came, they stood side by side. If they stood before the council, they stood together. They did not face the cold times alone. They did not face danger alone. They had the strength of each other. Ach was young, but he saw this strength. As well, he had a closeness with the son of his uncle, two summers younger than Ach. They were together so often that Ach had called him "Little Brother" since they were young. In time, Ach and his "Little Brother" would also have this strength of two.

As Ach looked behind him to the high end of the ridge, he could see the high trail running just beyond it. As the men travel to hunting areas, they use these high trails. They offer a good vantage point to watch out over the valley, looking for intruders. As the men walked, they kept a close eye on the trail itself, looking for tracks.

Sometimes the animals they hunted would walk along there. Other times, the men would see tracks of bear, or of wolf, themselves hunting along the trail. But most of all, the men kept watch for the tracks of other men.

Intruders came with different hearts. Other, more distant neighbors may cross into the valley, hunting, looking for what they might find. If their hearts were not dark, if they showed respect for the villages, they would not be harmed. But this was not exactly the same as being welcome. Sometimes the Rock men would let themselves be seen, watching from the high trails. The visitors would know the valley was not empty, it was not open to them. Usually, they would depart quietly to hunt elsewhere.

These visitors were not the ones the people feared. Sometimes, by one or by two, "Coyotes" would come. They came to steal. They came to take the women, and if they struggled, the women would sometimes be killed. The Coyotes would laugh. What sport it was to do as they pleased. There were places along the high trails where wood was piled, in places visible from the villages. The men, and many of the women, carried sticks to make fire. At the first site of dangerous intruders, they would light the signal fires to warn the others.

Allied as they were, whenever these Coyotes were seen, the men of the two valley clans joined quickly together. They would encircle the intruders and kill them. It's not good to allow Coyotes to escape. They will return home and talk of what they have found. Others may follow their path, to see what they may find, or brothers may come to avenge the dead ones.

In the time of Ach's grandfather, three such men had killed one of the daughters of the Cloud people. The men of the tribes surrounded them, and killed them. So angered was the girl's father that he and his brothers cut lodge poles and followed the men's tracks to the place where the thieves had entered the valley. They tied the poles together and stood them up. They tied the Coyote's dead bodies to them as a warning. The birds that eat death perched upon them for many days, a clear message to other such men. The memory of this message lingered. For many summers, no one crossed into the valley on that trail.

In Ach's time, the council was ruled by calmer heads. If black-hearted intruders are caught, they are killed as before. But now their bodies, their weapons, their clothes, all their possessions are dragged to an area with soft ground. The bodies are covered with dirt and rocks. Gone, quietly, as if they had never entered this valley. Their things are buried with them in case others from their tribes come looking. "Not here. We have seen no one." This may seem cowardly, but the elders said it will end the revenge killings, stop further fighting. When the men don't return, their families keep their brothers home, and tell them "it is not wise to steal from other men".

But today, Ach saw no tracks of men. Only small prints were visible in the dust of the trail. Hard to make out because of the dryness, but much smaller than a wolf and surely not a bear. But what? He wasn't sure if these were the tracks of food, but at least they were not the foot prints of danger. He would watch them as he walked, slowly along the high trail, arrows and spear at the ready. He didn't often hunt alone, but today he wasn't after dangerous game. Today a deer would be nice, or one of the goats from the mountain. Even a rabbit would be good, to feed him for today, stronger to hunt tomorrow. As he walked, he saw the small foot prints, and he wondered.

- o 0 o -

Names

Ach means "throwing stone", a round stone that fits nicely in the hand and can be thrown well. When Ach was small, his father knew he was smart, and called him "Little Fox". But when he was nearly grown, with summers numbering two hands and one, he would win the name he would wear as a man. When young boys join the hunt, they usually are too small for spears and bows. They are still too young to get in close to dangerous animals, and any hunter knows that animals are most dangerous when they are frightened, and hurt. So usually, the boys stay back. They watch, learn, and help to cut and carry meat if the hunt is successful.

On one of his early hunts, Ach walked with the men, quietly, searching the ground. One of the men in front spotted a large beast. It had curled teeth as long as a man's hand, coming from the sides of its snout. It was backed up against a steep drop, with nowhere to escape. Ach's father was nearest and threw his spear. Striking the beast, the spear entered, and bloodied him, but did not bring him down. The animal stumbled, frightened, and as he turned angrily towards the men, his hind feet found the edge of the drop. Over he went, tumbling as the men rushed to the edge to look. Frightened, injured and confused, this was the moment to finish him.

Ach's uncle made it first to the edge, and though he had been told to stay back, Ach rushed right up beside him. His uncle saw the beast just below them, on the steep slope where it had landed. The fall hadn't hurt the animal much, but it made it hard for him to attack the men, now above it on the hill. A lucky break for the men. Many have been killed when such a beast slices open their bellies with those long, curved teeth.

Ach's uncle raised his spear and prepared to throw. But just as he did this, the rocks at the edge of the drop gave way, and down his uncle slid, crashing, rolling, stopping right in front of the beast!

Their eyes met as the beast struggled to its feet, and prepared to kill him. Ach had always had a skill throwing stones, but before today, it mostly got him into trouble. No bow, no spear in his hands, he had only one stone. He saw the beast, and time stopped for him, his hand rose, the stone flew and caught the beast sharply, just atop its head. Ach's father saw this and knew the stunned beast may only be dazed for a moment, a few heart beats. He raised the spear his brother had dropped and threw, cutting deep into the animal's heart.

The uncle could not find his breath. One moment he saw nothing but death staring right into his eyes, the next, the stone stunned the animal, and the spear ended him. The others picked the Uncle up and found him to be uninjured. They cut up the animal while the Uncle sat and stared, legs too wobbly to stand.

That night, the uncle went before the village fire and said that the boy, who had been called "Little Fox", was ready for a new name, the name of a man. For his skill with stones, for stunning the animal, for thinking quickly and saving the life of his uncle, from this day the village will call him "Ach". But not the uncle, the uncle would call him "son". The uncle stood with his hands on the boy's shoulders and said "a man's strength comes from his father and from this day, Ach will have two."

-o0o-

Black Stones

One day, as Ach walked the high trail, he again saw the small footprints. As he followed along, looking at times into the valley, and at times up the slope for deer or goats, he frequently glanced down at the trail, at the tracks. Finally, the footprints crossed some smooth dust and made a clear impression. "Ha! A fox, of course," Ach thought. They were too small even for the cats that roamed the valley, and they were not the prints of a rabbit. Rabbits constantly dart from one hiding spot to another, hoping neither cats, nor eagles, nor wolves will spot them. These tracks, walking straight down the middle of the trail, were the foot prints of a fox!

As Ach looked at the dusty prints, he spotted something else unusual, a small, shiny, black stone. It was tiny, but it looked like a familiar kind of stone. Ach's cousin, the one he called "Little Brother", was a frequent maker of arrow points. He had a skill for it, he did it quickly and smoothly while the others were cutting and striking their fingers. He often used a brown colored "mother stone" that Ach's uncle had traded for some time ago. It was very rough around the edges, and almost as big as a man's head. The other's had no luck with it, so "Little Brother" had asked to try.

He was able to hold the stone, and strike it, just on the edge, with a round, hard stone. For him, it seemed easy to strike the large stone, and get a wide, flat piece to flake off the edge. He would then put the large mother stone down, and begin to shape and sharpen the flake. In no time, he would have a high quality arrow point, or spear point, depending on the size of the flake. You could hear him work, sinc, sinc the sound of a, properly struck, mother stone. In time, this became his name, Sinc.

But this black stone was different. It looked sharp even on its broken edge as it lay there in the dust. Ach took it to show to Sinc. They might be able to find more, and maybe it would make good points as well. The stone Sinc used now was good, but he only had one, and as he struck more flakes, it was harder to get good ones, especially ones large enough for spear points.

Ach took the small stone to Sinc. Sinc laughed at the tiny thing. He laughed, but he looked. "Hmmm," he said, "smooth like the brown mother stone, but yes, even though just broken, not shaped by hand, it is still sharp." "We must look for more," Sinc said.

And so the next time Ach headed up to that portion of the high trails, he took Sinc with him. They found the spot on the trail where Ach had found the stone, but searching, they found no more. The area up above the trail was high, and reached right up to the rim of the valley. The men did not usually travel there to hunt, because the grass and bushes there grew very low, only as high as a man's knee. This made it very hard for the men to find cover. Any deer or goats would seem them from far away, and leave long before the men could hunt them. Since the slope was steep and not easy to travel, the men had rarely climbed into that area.

But, curious, and eager to find more of the black stone, the boys began to search. They stuck to the center of the slope, where water would run on its path to the river, and looked for black. They slowly climbed and looked, occasionally finding tiny pieces like the first. Finally, they came to some large rocks, high above the trail. Here there were many small pieces, and even some sand that looked black. They must be getting close. Sinc used his walking stick to pry apart two thin stones standing together. There between them, they saw black.

The two stones were heavy, and nearly as tall as a man. As the boys pushed and pried, and kicked them, they placed a smaller stone between them at the top. Any time they made the stones move, the wedge stone slipped down, farther in between the tall ones, holding them apart. The boys began to see more and more black. They used other rocks to pound the wedge stone down, until at last, the two stones gave up and fell to the side. Under and behind them was an area of black rock about half as tall as a man, and about three handsb wide. Lots of stones, mother stones, broken pieces, side by side in the crack.

Sinc's eyes grew wide. He couldn't wait to try to make an arrow point. He sat right down on the tall rocks, now lying on the slope. He had some striking stones in a pouch and got them out. He picked up a small mother stone and struck it, sinc, sinc, and a beautiful, long piece flaked off. He began to break the edges, and quickly shaped and sharpened it into a fine arrow point. He wrapped a piece of skin around it, so he wouldn't cut his fingers, and tried to break it. It held firm. He dropped it, and then threw it down on one of the flat stones. Instead of shattering, it only chipped on the edge that struck rock, and the chipped place was just as sharp as the shaped edges!

This stone was fantastic! Sinc looked at Ach with wide eyes, "Ach, this is important! I can make <u>many</u> points with these stones." The boys gathered several more mother stones, and started the long walk back to the village. Sitting, hidden, as he had been all afternoon, the fox watched the boys hurry away. They were eager to show their fathers what they had found.

- o 0 o -

Trading

A stream runs down the valley. It starts well up above the Cloud village, and runs past the Rock village, all the way through the long valley and into the river. The river is quite a distance, and usually when hunting, the men do not travel that far. Schut and Schut-Tah, Ach's father and uncle, had been there before, seeking other villages to trade with, or when looking for wives. One day, two of the Cloud men were returning from a long trip to the river when they stopped at the Rock village. They said they had met a man from down river.

When meeting other tribes, communication is often difficult as most of their words are different. But by making signs and exchanging looks and expressions, the Cloud and Rock people could communicate with outsiders when needed. Of course, the words of Cloud people and the Rock people were nearly the same, and so between them, speaking was easy.

These two Cloud men said that the man they met was a trader. He had signed that he was headed back down river, but that he would return to that spot, at the time of the next full moon. At the village fire, the Old Man spoke to the Rock people. They made a plan to travel with the Cloud people, to meet the trader and see what they could trade.

Sinc had been using the new-found black stones to make arrow points, and a few spear points. Points were always good to trade. Other tribes also struggled when trying to make fine points, the natural skill that Sinc had wasn't common. Sinc showed these points to his father, Schut-Tah, and they decided to take them to the traders.

Schut and Ach had been lucky at their hunting during the cold times. They killed two nice elk and the women had prepared their skins well, good for trading. One of the cloud men had a daughter of the age to go with a man, he would take her along. The Rock people sometimes went to the Cloud people when looking for a woman, but several of the families there had brothers or fathers in the other tribe, so usually both tribes would go down to the river and look to more distant villages for their women.

Seeing this girl got Schut to thinking. Ach's summers now numbered three hands. Schut had a staff which represented his lodge. He had carved a mark in it when each of his children was born, and carved a small mark for each of their summers, the same way many families kept track of such things. Three hands, time for Ach to take a woman, time for him to start his own lodge. Schut-Tah saw his brother looking at the marks on the staff. Schut smiled and gave him a wink, but said nothing to Ach. Schut-Tah gave two of the nice spear points that Sinc had made, to Schut. Those points, with the two nice elk skins, might make a good trade for a woman.

At the turn of the moon, it was time for the trader to return. The men of both tribes gathered their items and prepared for the walk down to the river. The Cloud man with the daughter asked her to come along with him. Although the girl had no idea what it meant to make this journey, her mother did, as did all of the women. This was the way. Men sometimes took their daughters to such gatherings. The father would look for other men who were looking for a woman, and who looked like they would care for her. When Ach and Schut would stand before the group, showing their elk skins and the fine spear points, this would show that they were skillful men, good men, good fathers. A father had no easy desire to give away his daughter, but if he could satisfy himself that she would go to a good man, to a strong village, he would arrange it.

At the river, the traders were just arriving. The groups planned to stay there for perhaps two or three nights, until the trading and the talking were done. On the first day, the traders spread three or four large skins on the ground. Several kinds of goods were available, wood for spear shafts, skins, tools made of bone, scrapers for hides, water skins, and of course, young women. Those who brought things would sit around the skins, and wait for the right moment to trade.

In Ach's valley, there were trees that produced good wood for arrow shafts. But, because they were high in the valley, the Rock people didn't have good, long shafts for spears. Sinc noticed that one of the men had brought some spear shaft wood that was very long, more than twice the length of a man. He had never seen spears that long. He tried to ask the man about it, but his words were too different. The man just signed that the wood could be cut.

But Sinc was thinking differently. He remembered the angry beast that almost killed his father. The men would have been safer if they could have stuck the animal with long spears, from a greater distance. Sinc spoke to Schut-Tah. They put two of the nice spear points down on the skins, and the man gave them a hand and three of the long shafts, and two hands of normal spear shafts for them. A good trade, Schut-Tah was proud of his son.

And then, Schut rose and approached the skins. He motioned for Ach to rise and join him, which he did. As Ach stood at the edge of the skins, Schut spread out one of the nice elk skins. He began to look around the group, in a way that the fathers there understood. Schut had been looking at the several girls all morning, and felt that two or three of them could make good candidates. He spread the second elk skin out for the men to examine, and as he did so, Ach wondered what his father was trying to trade for. Schut still had not told him of his plan. The men sitting around the skins sensed this, and began to chuckle.

As Schut placed one of the nice spear points down on the skins, Schut-Tah rose to stand beside his brother, and Sinc rose to stand beside Ach. Finally, it sunk in, Ach realized what was going on. His face got red, which caused the men to chuckle even more. When Schut put the second spear point down, he had the whole group's attention. Standing together, the four men looked like a strong family group, a group that could hunt, and make fine weapons. These were men who would care for a young woman. The fathers in the group stood up, first one, and then quickly the others. Several brought their daughters forward.

Schut now motioned for Ach to step back with him for a moment, so they could talk. Ach was about to explode, with embarrassment, with fear, with excitement. Schut pointed, in a way the other men could not see, to one of the young girls. She looked healthy, she looked strong, and she looked smart. Ach agreed with a nod of his head. Schut walked out onto the skins and looked at her father. The father took the girl's hand and brought her forward. Sinc, standing near, put something into Ach's hand. Ach looked, it was a necklace, made with a small black arrow point. Sinc nodded, and motioned to the girl.

Ach walked out onto the skins. He walked to the girl and placed the necklace around her neck. He held out his hand. Slowly, just as embarrassed as Ach was, she took his hand. As they walked back to the edge of the skins, the deal was done. Ach had taken a wife. The girl's father took Ach's hand and looked into his eyes. Without words, he asked Ach to take good care of his daughter.

Her name was Sana. It was the name of the first flowers to be seen in spring. Even before the first blades of grass began to grow, the small, light blue sana would be seen all through the valley. With the trading completed, the Rock people and the Cloud people gathered their things and began the long walk back up the valley.

The Cloud man had not seen a man he felt worthy of his daughter. So, without ever being sure why he had taken her along, she followed him back home. As Sinc and Schut-Tah had known about the plan to get Ach a woman, so had Ach's mother. She was back home, preparing to welcome a new daughter into their lodge.

As the group walked up the valley trail, toward the Rock and Cloud villages, they carried the fruits of their trading. Well, they carried the many shafts of the normal spears, and Sinc's friend from the Cloud people helped him carry the long shafts, but the other item they took in trade *walked*. Sana, the young woman, the new wife of Ach, walked along with the group, nervous, not knowing what to expect of her new village, her new family. She walked with the daughter of the Cloud man, who began to teach her some of the words they spoke. Sana was smart, and by signing, and learning the beginnings of their language, she would soon communicate well with the valley people.

Ach's mother, Sun-Ti, had some of the small boys keep watch for the men on the trail. They ran to her when they sighted the group, and she gathered the women of the village together. "Today, we welcome a new wife for my son," Sun-Ti said, "Hold out your hands to her, speak kind words, let her know the village will take her in." This was an exciting day for the village. Even though she had only called to the women, all of the small children came as well. If the small children came, then the older ones must come also, and soon everyone, all the men, even the Old Man, stood along the sides of the trail to welcome the new woman.

As the party approached the Rock village, they saw the people assembled there. Ach took the hand of his new wife, and led her to them. He spoke in a loud voice so all could hear, "I am Ach," which they all knew of course, "I have taken a wife," which they also knew by now. "Her name is Sana." The village greeted her, and laughed at the red face of Ach. They all touched her hands to let her know they accepted her, and that she would now be one of the Rock people, a member of the larger family that was the village. She felt at ease, welcome, as the women lead her away. They would show her the lodge where she would sleep. They would show where they did their work, cleaning skins, cutting and drying meat, picking and drying berries. Now, she was one of them.

-o0o-

Long Spears

The name of Ach's father was Schut, which means "Spear". Schut's brother, Ach's uncle, was named Schut-Tah, "Spear Point". When they were old enough, ready for a man's name, they already had a reputation of working together, of supporting each other. By then, their father was gone, killed as stones and white cover slid down the mountain in the cold. But even though the boy's father was gone, their grandfather was still alive.

Since the grandfather's woman was also gone, and he had been alone in his lodge, he had moved the two boys and their mother in with him. He knew that his time was short, as his summers had already reached hands of one hand and four. He stood before the village fire and asked the Rock people to call the boys by these new names, "Schut and Schut-Tah." They were names of respect, and he believed the names would help the boys to work together, to take care of each other. The grandfather knew that when he was gone, if the mother was still alive, she would need to find a new man. The boys, now young men, would be on their own. The grandfather used his last few summers to prepare them.

Prepare them well he did. Schut and Schut-Tah were fine, strong men, well respected by their village. In addition, they had each raised fine, strong sons, smart sons, skilled hunters and makers of weapons. Such men, and boys, were of great value to a village. For when any lodge hunted well, and brought meat back to the village, all shared it. All the women helped to skin, and cut and dry, and all ate. This is what kept the village strong. If one lodge was unlucky with its hunt, another would succeed. It was important to share, so that all the men would be strong, to hunt, and to defend the village. The stronger the men were, the greater the chances that all the village would make it through the cold times.

The new black stones that Ach and Sinc had found brought good luck to the Rock people. The points they made were used to make many arrows and spears. The boys also made the new, long spears with the long shafts Sinc had traded for. These better arrows and spears would improve the hunting of all the Rock men.

The Long Spears would help them with dangerous game like bear or beasts. It was always dangerous to take such game and to make it safer for the men would mean fewer injuries, maybe fewer deaths. When winters were difficult, the death of one of the men usually was followed by the deaths of others, young children, women, or the old ones. Removing one healthy man could mean less food gathered, fewer skins to keep warm, and it put many in the village at risk. In difficult winters, those on the edge sometimes did not come through.

So even though Ten-Ha, grand-father of Schut and Schut-Tah, great-grand-father to Ach and Sinc, had been gone for many, many summers, his teaching of his grandsons, and their teaching of his great-grand-sons still helped the Rock people, still kept them strong. Ten-Ha's name was a funny one, it actually means "grand-son". Though Schut did not know the story of how his grand-father got his name, he thought that Ten-Ha might also have been raised by his own grand-father.

Thus it was with the Rock people, and the Cloud people. For men, the lessons of hunting, of defending the tribe, of being fathers, were passed from one generation to another. The same was true for the women, passing the lessons of children, gathering food, feeding the tribe. This was what kept the families and the village alive and strong. By finding the new black stones, Ach and Sinc had done something that would help their people for many, many summers. By making the Long Spears, and by the uses they would later find for them, the two allied tribes would be strong and healthy, and would be _known_ to be, for a long time to come.

-o0o-

Warning

Ach enjoyed walking the high trails. He enjoyed the view down the long valley. At this time of year, he enjoyed the first cool air of the coming cold time. There was still game to hunt high on the valley walls, the cold had not yet pushed the animals down into the lower parts of the valley. Ach walked along the high trail, quietly, looking for signs of deer or goats, and looking for the foot prints of the fox.

On the path, well up ahead of him, he saw for the first time, the fox, sitting on the edge of the trail. The fox sat, looking down the steep slope into the valley. This looked strange to Ach. Any prey that might interest the fox would be way too far away if it were down in the valley. The fox turned and saw Ach, but even stranger, he went back to looking into the valley. As Ach approached, finally, the fox turned, and disappeared into the low bushes.

Seeing this unusual behavior, Ach went to the place the fox had been sitting, and himself sat down to look into the valley. He wondered if he would be able to see what the fox had been watching. For some time, his eyes searched, first on the valley wall just beneath him, and then further down, to the valley floor. His eyes saw nothing unusual, and began to look further away, down the valley. There, far below him, on the trail by the stream that flowed along the valley floor, he saw something moving. It was a man. He could not tell if he was Rock or Cloud, but he could tell that he was afraid.

The man would run for some distance, and then, from behind a tree or rock, he would look back down the valley, as if to see who followed. As Ach looked on, the man left the stream trail and began to head up the side of the valley, toward Ach. This behavior was quite puzzling. Why was the man running, why leave the trail and head up the valley wall? And then it came to Ach, "the signal fires!" One of the fire places was near where Ach was sitting. Was the man coming to light it? Had he seen trouble?

Ach moved to a place beside a bush, where the man might see him, but others down the valley would not. "Oooooooowwweeeee," he called out, and well down the slope, the running man stopped in his tracks. Ach gave a whistle and waved his arm so the man would see him. The man did, and began to point back down the valley. Indeed, he had seen trouble. Ach pointed toward the place of the signal fire. The man saw this, and he also pointed to it, several times, quickly.

That was it, he meant to light the fire. In all of Ach's summers, he had never seen the lighting of the signal fires. They were only used in times of great danger. He waved again, and moved quickly along the high trail to meet the man there. By the time the Cloud man made it up to the high place, Ach had a small fire started, off to the side. Gasping for breath, the man said the word that meant "*Raiders.*" Ach turned, and lit the signal fire.

-o0o-

Running Birds

With Raiders in the valley, the Cloud and Rock men needed to act quickly. They met at the place of the council fire and began to talk. The Old Man said that the women should take their stored food out of the lodges and hide it. They should also hide the children and themselves. He said that the men must go and meet the raiders, and that if they fought bravely, they would turn the raiders away. But if things went badly, the women would have to be prepared. They must be hidden away until the raiders left, and must have enough stored food to make it through the cold time. All must prepare.

The Old Man spoke of the small, running birds that live in the valley. These birds did not usually fly, but ran about on the ground, looking for food. When the birds saw a hunter approaching, whether man, or cat, or fox, the birds would gather together in the grass and hide. As the hunter got closer, the birds would wait until the hunter was almost stepping on them, and then, "Brrrrrrrrrrrrrrrrrrrrr," all would fly up at once, and in all directions.

Even if the hunter was a cat, though cats have no equal in catching small, fast game, the surprise of the sudden flight would confuse and frighten. The birds would get away. While hunting, many of the men had been laughed at by their companions for the fright they showed as the birds had exploded into flight at their feet. The Old Man said this kind of surprise, this kind of quick action would be needed to defeat the raiders.

The Old Man also spoke of the way the birds acted as one. All the Cloud Men and all the Rock Men would need to act, and think, as one. This was the time when the two villages, acting together, most needed their power of two.

He looked at Sinc, and told him to go and get the long spears he had made. He told four of the younger boys to move, quietly, down the valley, to watch the raiders, but not to be seen. Two would keep their eyes on the raiders, and two would run back to the Old Man to report. He told the Wolf and the Rock Men to go, and gather their spears and bows. When they returned, he would lay out his plan.

As the boys reported the position of the raiders, the Old Man made a plan to put the village men in their path. He would pick a position just down the valley, before the trail reached the Rock village. He wanted this fight to take place away from the homes of his people. He could not risk that the lodges may be destroyed or burned in the fight. The cold times were coming. People without warm lodges would die.

The Old Man believed that the raiders would come strong, and would meet the village men with several raiders out front, most likely including the leader. If they spoke, their leader would do the talking. The Old Man also believed that the raiders would feel that they were much stronger then the village men. He hoped to use their arrogance against them.

As the Old Man had told them, the village men placed themselves on the trail. The Wolf, Schut, Schut-Tah, and two other Cloud men stood at front. Each held a spear in his weak hand. Holding the spears like this looked timid, the spears were not in the strong hand, not held high over the shoulder ready to throw. The spears would look like they were just being carried.

Just behind the village front-men was another hand of men. The raider leader would see that these "second-men" were not the leaders of the village, and would not expect trouble from them. Again, the Old Man hoped that the raiders would feel powerful and arrogant in the face of this "*weak*" group of men.

Further behind the "front-men" were two other groups of valley men, hidden in the bushes. One group off to each side, each of these men had bows and a hand of arrows at the ready. At the right time, they would step out, and have a clear view of the place where the Old Man hoped the raiders would be standing.

The two watchers came running down the path, the raiders would not be far behind. The Old Man signaled for all to be ready, then hid himself to watch, and wait.

- o 0 o -

Weakness

When the raiders appeared, they saw the village men standing in the path. They laughed at this pathetic group sent out to chase them away. As the Old Man expected, the leader with four others beside him, stepped out in front, with about two hands of other men behind them. The raiders were indeed brave. They had traveled into several of the valleys, taken what they wanted from several villages, and they were well armed. They felt no fear from the one hand of village front-men, and the one hand of smaller men "hiding" behind them.

The leader spoke. His words were too different to understand, but that didn't matter. The men all knew that he said something like, "give us what we want, stay out of our way, and perhaps, we will not kill you." He said something that made the rest of the raiders laugh hard, and when he did, Schut and the Wolf knew it was time for the birds to fly.

The village front-men started to bend their bodies down, looking as if they were laying their spears down on the ground, looking as if they were surrendering. But suddenly the eyes of the raider leader grew wide. The items in the valley front-men's hands were not their normal spears, they were just holding the front end of the much longer spears, held by the men behind them! The back-men, with the long spears well in hand, burst forward, catching the raiders off guard.

The raider leader was struck in the chest by one of the spears. He wore hard skins to protect himself, but the spear shaft bent and flexed. The spear point slid off the top of the chest skins, slicing through his throat and on through the side of his neck. Blood sprayed over the faces of the men beside him. All were caught, surprised, as the leader grabbed his throat, gasped for air, and went down. The other long spears, thrust like lances, found the other raider front-men, as the valley back-men drove forward. Then, the valley bowmen stepped out from their hiding places and filled the sky with arrows.

The two hands of raiders standing behind the leader were terrified. Some dropped from arrows, and others turned to run. Arrows caught some of the runners as the Wolf, Schut and the other valley front-men picked up their normal spears, hidden beside them on the ground, and ran into the fight.

But it was no real fight. The raiders were caught with their eyes wide and their faces full of fear. Their leader and three of their front-men lay dead, the fifth was screaming in pain. Of the two hands of raiders behind, arrows caught a hand and three. Three lay dead, three lay screaming, and two tried to crawl away. Schut and the Wolf caught the ones that ran. The Old Man signed for the boys to silence the screaming ones, and the ones crawling away. He sent other men down the path, to see if the raiders had boys or women behind them on the trail.

The Valley Men found a few boys hiding down the trail. The Old Man said to let them go. If they made it back to their villages alive, they would tell the story of this day. The birds had won. With none of the valley men hurt, the raiders were defeated. Beaten by a small group that was smart, that was prepared, and that was led by a wise Old Man.

That night, at the council fire, the Old Man spoke of the bravery of the Valley Men. Their plan was a simple one, acted out with great surprise. But he warned them, "Do not find arrogance in this victory. It was arrogance that caused the raiders to come in close, their foolishness left them dead." He reminded them all that the defeat would be a disaster for the raider's villages. Without men to hunt, many in the villages would be hungry. The cold would push them to the edge of life, and many would not come through.

- o 0 o -

A Woman for Sinc

As it does every year, the cold time in the valley passed. The Rock and the Cloud people had come through well. Their preparations, the drying and storing of food, had been good. The repairs to their lodges had been done before the tough weather. Hunting well and hunting safely meant the men had time for such repairs and preparation. Hunting done early, instead of in the depths of the cold time, meant that the women were better prepared. It meant that their lodges, and their families were warm, and their babies were well fed. It meant that the men did not have to risk going out when the weather was at its worst.

All these things made life better for the tribes. Finding the new black stones, making long spears, defending the villages from the raiders, had made a huge difference. What would winter have been like if their food had been stolen? If several men had been injured, the rest would have had to risk the bad weather to find food, no choice. And how many lodges might have been damaged in a fight? How would the men have repaired them if they were off on a desperate search for food? The Old Man had told the council fire that many, many from the two tribes might not have made it through.

Life was their reward. For working together as one, for finding and making new weapons, for taking the knowledge of the old ones, and passing it to the young ones, for passing the lessons of fathers to sons, and of mothers to daughters. This held the villages together. This brought them life.

As the weather warmed and the grass began to grow, Schut-Tah began to look at Sinc. A season had passed since Ach took a wife, now Schut-Tah thought about a wife for his son. Without speaking about it to Sinc, Schut-Tah began to gather things he might trade for a girl. He told Schut of his idea. His brother smiled and agreed. At the time of the long day, at mid-summer, there would be trading.

When Schut-Tah had taken a wife, she had come from down river, where the water slowed and became very wide. So, for Sinc, maybe it would be best to go up river. There were villages there, and most likely, girls.

"The Wolf," the leader of the Cloud people, was not exactly the man's name. Instead, the elders of the Cloud village would select a man to be called "The Wolf." In times of trouble, like when the raiders came, it was this "Wolf" who would lead the Cloud men to stand with the Rock men, to defend the tribes. The Wolf would also lead the hunters, and make sure the lessons were passed on to the boys. The man who was now the Wolf had been injured a few summers ago. For a time, the elders appointed a new "Wolf". But the man had healed well, and since he was widely respected, not only by the Cloud people but by the Rock village as well, the elders had asked him to resume his role as "The Wolf".

Schut and Schut-Tah thought this was good. This man was about their same age, and they had known him as boys. They got along well with him, and this made the relationship between the Rocks and Clouds even stronger. This friendship would be a good thing, because the Wolf had a daughter. She was about the same age… as Sinc.

She was a tall girl, and strong. She had a smart look, and had always been at the side of her mother, who was a leader among the Cloud women. This meant that she had heard many of the lessons of the women. She was always around when new things were to be learned. It would make her a good wife and a strong asset to a new village when she went with a man.

The usual way of choosing a woman for a young man was the way it had been done for Ach. That is, except for the part about not telling him in advance, that was Schut's idea. But that was the way, to go and select a woman, one from a different village, usually one the boy had never met before. Usually.

This time, as the time of the long day approached, Schut-Tah called Sinc aside to talk. He told Sinc of the trading. This Sinc knew, he was already preparing several points and stone tools to trade. Then

Schut-Tah told Sinc that it was time for him to take a wife, and that, if they could find a good young woman at the trading, they would bring her home to the Rock village.

Schut-Tah did not understand the look on Sinc's face. It was not the red, embarrassed look he had seen on Ach's face. Sinc was troubled. His father asked what was wrong. "Father," Sinc said, "I am not ready to take a woman…from the traders." He paused, and struggled with his words. "I have in my mind…another woman," Sinc said. She is…," he cleared his throat, "Ayea, the daughter of the Wolf." Surprised, Schut-Tah raised his eye brows. "Is this so?" he asked. "Yes," Sinc said. "Does she know this?" Schut-Tah asked, not sure that he wanted to know the answer. "Yes," Sinc said.

"Hmmm," Schut-Tah responded, "This could be difficult. I will talk about it, with Schut, and with the Old Man". Schut-Tah tried to reassure his son, "Do not worry, you are a fine young man. The Wolf knows this." Sinc allowed himself to breathe. He had no idea how his father would react. Sinc cared for Ayea, he had seen her at many council fires. And, she had seen him. They had caught each other's eyes several times, each time quickly looking away, each glancing about, hoping that no one else had noticed.

The moon was high, and nearly full. At each full moon in the warm times, the Rock and the Cloud people met at the place of the Council Fire. In times of trouble, the villages would meet there, as they had when the raiders came. But when there was no trouble, they met at the full moon to tell stories, to talk of hunting, the things neighbors usually speak of. This time, Schut-Tah and Sinc approached it with nervousness. They brought with them the things that they planned to trade for the girl. Schut and the Old Man came with them, as did the rest of the village.

As Schut-Tah approached the place of the Council Fire, he asked his woman, Sinc's mother, to come with him. Sinc handed him the things that he and Sinc had planned to trade. Schut-Tah asked Sinc to go and help the other boys make the fire, as he usually did. Schut-Tah saw the Wolf, and asked if they might speak. The Wolf said "yes, we will speak at the fire," but Schut-Tah motioned that he would like to speak away from the others. He signed for the wife of the Wolf to join them.

As Schut and the Old Man had recommended, he began to tell the whole story to the Wolf, about Sinc needing a woman, about their idea to trade. The Wolf wondered why Schut-Tah started by telling of the plan to go and meet the traders. He knew this already, as he planned to go with the Rock people, but he listened patiently. And then, Schut-Tah told about Sinc's idea, that his woman should be Ayea. The Wolf now saw the things that Schut-Tah had brought to trade. With no words in his look, he asked to speak with his wife, Ayea's mother, alone.

It was time for the fire to begin, so Schut-Tah took his place and sat down. He had spread skins on the ground where he and his woman would sit, as had the other men around the fire. As there was no trouble in the valley, this Council Fire was relaxed. Some men told hunting stories. Some had questions, about tying spear-points to shafts, or making other tools. The talking went on for a while, as it usually did. This meeting happened once in a full moon, and only in the warm times, so there was usually a lot to catch up on.

Finally, the Wolf rose to speak. "All know that I have a daughter", his firm voice reached across the group. "A fine young woman, and nearly the age to go to a man." He paused, as all fell silent to listen. "Tonight, at the first full moon of the warm time, a father has come to me. He asks to trade for my daughter. He will trade two fine elk skins, three black spear points and three black scraping tools for this fine young girl, so cared for by her mother, and by me." Schut-Tah began to squirm, thinking perhaps he had made a mistake. Sinc could not breathe. Ayea, surprised by all of this, was afraid to move. Nothing, but the crackling of the fire, could be heard.

Apparently, Ayea's mother had seen the eyes of Sinc and Ayea at the Council Fires. She knew what this meant. As they spoke prior to the fire, she had told this to the Wolf. He continued, "I have thought about this trade. I have spoken to my woman, and I have decided... There will be <u>no trade</u>!" he said in a loud, booming voice that shattered the silence. The entire group gasped. But, the Old Man stood up, and with him stood Schut. The Wolf had nodded to them, and given a wink, before he began to speak. They knew what was happening.

"Sinc, stand up!" boomed the Wolf, "Ayea, stand!" "I have decided that tonight, there will be no trade…" The whole group held its breath. Even the crickets were afraid to make a sound. "Because, the hand of Ayea…will be a gift!" The people of both villages jumped to their feet. The men cheered for Sinc, the women hugged Ayea. Schut-Tah's knees were again wobbly, but this time he managed to stand. The Wolf came to Schut-Tah and took his hand. It was the hand of friendship, and now, of family.

"The skins and other things that Sinc brought to trade will also be gifts, to Ayea, for her new lodge," the Wolf said. All knew the Wolf cared for his daughter. All knew that it's difficult for a father, and mother, to give away a daughter, especially to a village far away. Parents always knew, they may not see their daughter again. But now, Ayea would be with a man she cared for, and who cared for her. Even better, they would live in a village nearby, one that the Cloud people visited frequently. The Old Man smiled and took strongly the hand of the Wolf. This was another lace, among the many, that tied the two villages together.

-o0o-

The Girl

The original plan to walk up-river to trade had included finding a woman for Sinc. Now that Sinc had a woman, that plan had changed. But life had been good to the Rock people. The cold times had not stressed them, all were healthy. Instead of scurrying about during the early warm time, trying to find food, they were still eating the leftover food they had stored for the cold times. This meant they had time to think about trading, time to gather items that other traders might want. So it was decided, even though Sinc did not need a woman, the Rock men would go trading anyway. When it was time, they gathered their skins, tools, arrows, arrow points and spear points, and began the long walk.

It takes a long day of walking to get from the Rock village down to the end of the valley, to the river. There the group spread skins, made a cooking fire and rested for the night. This place was the same spot where Ach had traded for Sana. In the early morning, they gathered their things and set off again. After another long day's walk upstream, they came to a gathering of men at the side of the river. They arrived in darkness, but the people gathered had built a large fire and all were talking and signing, excited about the trading. The Rock men picked a spot to sleep and spread out their skins.

The weather was good. The morning was cool, but the sky was a beautiful blue and the air warmed quickly. With no pressure to select a woman to take home, the Rock men relaxed and wandered around the camp, looking at the goods on display, and looking at the people. At the earlier trading, when Ach found Sana, the group was friendlier. That trader was one they had seen before, from down river. This time, the same trader was there, but there were many other people, from far villages, that the Rock men did not know. Some looked as if they might be Coyotes. Schut and Schut-Tah decided to keep an eye on them.

The trading began as before. Various goods were brought to the edges of the large skins. The people would look, and perhaps offer to trade. There were several women at the gathering. Some were young, and their fathers looked at the crowd, to see which men might be suitable. One of the girls looked quite young. A man signed to Schut-Tah that she was available. Schut-Tah only understood a few of his words, but it seemed that he was her uncle. Her father was gone, so the uncle had moved her and her mother into his lodge.

Schut-Tah mentioned this to Schut. Both were troubled that the uncle would offer the girl at such an early age. She had, they guessed, only summers numbering two hands and one, or maybe two. She should stay with her mother for at least another two or three summers. Since the Rock men had not expressed an interest in her, the uncle had continued around the camp. Finally, he stopped in front of the men who looked like Coyotes. Schut and Schut-Tah had a bad feeling about this. The uncle seemed too willing to trade her. They feared he would not look out for her. If he traded her to the Coyotes, they might just play with her for a while, and then trade her again, to who knows where.

This seemed wrong to the brothers, and they thought about what to do. Sinc and Ach heard their concerns and joined the discussion. Ach asked, "What if we trade for her, and take her home with us?" But Schut had another idea. He suggested that he and Ach put their items together and make the uncle an offer. They would ask the uncle to take their skins and points now, but take the girl home with him. She would stay with her mother for two summers more, and then Ach would come for her.

The Rock men sometimes took more than one woman, especially when times were good, as they were now. And besides, the life of a woman was hard. When babies came, or winters were tough, sometimes the women died. Many of the Rock men had lost a wife. By making this trade for the girl, if the times remained good, and the tribe remained healthy, Ach would have a second woman, and would be the father of many babies. If times were harder, Schut would help him to hunt, so he could care for and feed both women. Ach's face was red again.

Schut and Schut-Tah found the uncle, and with the help of the trader, who knew more of the uncle's words, the men made a deal. The uncle would be rid of the girl, but not right away. And he would have nice skins, arrow points and arrows to take with him, to make his lodge warm, to make his hunting more successful. He agreed to take the girl back home, and signed to Ach the way to find the village. In two summers, Ach would come for her. Sinc had made a second necklace for Ach, with a small arrow point that matched the one that Sana wore. Ach put the necklace on the girl's neck and told her his name. "Ach", he said. Schut-Tah looked the uncle in the eyes, and took his hand firmly. The uncle understood, he must honor their agreement.

Her name was Cree. She was named for a sound made by some of the birds that come to the valley in the warm times. They make many sounds, different, interesting sounds. They have long tails and are bigger than many birds, but still much smaller than crows. Their feathers are shiny, as black as the night sky with no moon. Cree's hair was black, and shiny, and so she was named for these birds. Cree's father was gone, and so her mother was alone. Cree and her mother had moved in with her father's brother, the uncle, when the father died. They now lived with him and "Crow Woman".

Their lodge was small and crowded, and Crow Woman ran it with all the grace and caring of an angry crow. Cree had only thought this name for her, she would never dare say it aloud. There were three other children in the lodge, all from Crow Woman. She worked hard to feed them and did not see Cree and her mother as potential helpers, but as just adding to the size of the family. She did not say so, but she wanted them out. She did not say so, because it was the obligation of a man to take in the woman and children of his dead brother. She did not say so, but Cree and her mother knew she thought so.

Crow Woman was not happy when the uncle returned with the girl. She did not think the skins were enough, and the arrows and spear points meant nothing to her. Sometimes, in the warm times, Cree would sleep outside the lodge at night, so she did not have to listen to the squawking of the "crow".

- o 0 o -

The Long Walk

The uncle did his best, but the winter was hard. Since he had no father, and had lost his brother, the survival of the house was up to him, alone. It meant that a tough winter might mean that some were lost. There was always that risk, from injury, cold, or sickness, but with only one man to hunt, starvation may visit as well. The cold times were always that way.

But this time it was bad. Crow Woman watched as the whole group became weaker. One day, when the uncle was away, searching for any animals that had not left the valley when the white cover came, Crow Woman rose to her feet. Decided. She would not wait to see who would die first. She would not share food any longer with the wife and daughter of the dead brother, not if it meant her own children would die. Decided.

She took Cree and her mother by the arms and pulled them out into the cold. Cree resisted, pulling her mom back, but Crow Woman persisted. She pushed the two out, in a way that was very clear to the mom. They would have to go, but where? The other houses in the village had the same trouble. Their women seemed to know what was happening, all faces were turned away, no lodge doors were opened. Cree and her mom would have to leave the village, with heavy white cover on the ground. Death would walk with them.

Confused and upset, Cree asked her mother what was happening, why they had been pushed out. The mom, who had already been eating less, was already weak. She didn't reply, but looked about with her eyes, trying to decide what to do. The girl felt the shiny stone necklace against her skin. She touched it, and then pulled it out to look at it. As the mother saw it, the girl asked "Ach?"

Before leaving the trading, Ach had signed to Cree about his home. He had drawn in the dirt, showing her. They would walk down their valley, to the river, then turn and follow the water downstream. Did he say to cross two valleys, or three, she couldn't remember. The mother looked at the sky. The clouds were so heavy she couldn't tell how high the sun was. She looked down at the black stone. "Ach," she said. Their only hope. They turned, and began to walk.

When they reached the river, it had grown so dark that it was dangerous to go further. They found a place near a large rock that might offer shelter from the wind. They sat down, huddled together, and wrapped their skins around them as best they could. With the cold shaking their bodies, they drifted in and out of sleep.

As dawn approached, the girl was startled awake. She couldn't feel her feet, and her fingers would barely move. She asked her mother if she was alright, but there was no response. With the first light of the sun, Cree knew that she was now alone. There by the rock, the cold, the hunger, had taken her mother. All alone, she looked again at the stone necklace. To keep herself warm, she took some of the clothes her mother would no longer need, and began again, to walk.

- o 0 o -

The Wolf

Cree did not remember how many valleys she was supposed to cross, and walking through darkness, she didn't know how many she might have crossed already. She began to fear that she had gone too far. She feared that she had not gone far enough. She feared stopping and resting. She feared that she, like her mother, would not survive. She was starving, and freezing, and lost.

Had she not taken some of her mother's skins, she would not have made it this far. She was deeply saddened at the loss of her mother. But she dare not grieve, dare not break down, death would catch her if she did, and so she walked on. It was in this state, struggling on with her last bit of strength, that she thought she saw a man. Fearful of strangers, but even more fearful of the bitter cold, she hurried forward.

The man had made a small shelter to sleep in as he waited. He waited for some other Cloud men who were out hunting. At his small camp by the river, he cooked some meat on a fire. Seeing him, seeing the fire, smelling the food, she rushed so quickly that she fell in the deep white cover. When he heard this noise, he turned and saw her. He quickly realized that she was very young, and alone. He could also see how near death she was. He held out his hands, to show he was friendly, hands open and empty. She stumbled again, and he lifted her to her feet.

Out of breath, weak, and paralyzed with fear, she tried to speak. Her mouth opened, but no words came. She managed to make just a sound, "Aa," she gasped. And then, she thought again about the small black arrow point on her necklace, the one that Ach had given her. She managed to pull it out and show the man. "Aaa," again she tried to speak, "Aaa." But this man was a friend. He had seen the arrow point worn by Sana, just like this one. He knew that Ach had traded for another woman, a young girl. This man was "the Wolf".

He spoke quickly to her, but she did not understand. He said he knew Ach, "Ach!" she finally managed to say. He continued speaking, but she understood nothing. But as he lifted her and carried her to the fire, as he covered her with warm skins, as he put warm food into her hands, she understood. She understood that she would live. She ate some meat and some dried berries, and then, warm and safe in the hands of the Wolf, she fell into a deep sleep.

When morning came, the Wolf fed her again, and gave her water. He spoke and spoke, and she understood nothing, but her mood was high. He motioned for her to come with him along the river bank, to a clear place where a stream entered the river. There, way up the valley, where the sun first shines on the rocks, a tiny wisp of smoke could be seen. "Ach," he said pointing, "Ach!" She understood. He explained that he could not leave that place, until his friends returned, and again he wasted his breath, as she did not know his words.

The Wolf walked up the stream a little ways, and showed the girl where to cross. He signed for her to stay by the stream. He signed the location of the sun, and then showed how it would move across the sky. She understood: stay by the stream, and by the time the sun set, she should reach Ach and the Rock village. But more than that, with warm food in her stomach, and with dried meat and berries in a pouch the Wolf had given her, she understood that she would survive. She waved to the Wolf, and thanked him in words he did not understand, and began to walk up the path.

-o0o-

The Trail of the Fox

II

A New Lodge

When Ach introduced his new wife, Sana, to the family of the Rock village, it was time to begin work on a new "lodge" for the new young family. Now, a "lodge" is not necessarily just a house to live in. A lodge is a house, but it is also a "family". In this case, Sana joined the "lodge" of Ach, even though Ach didn't have his own house yet. So, a place must be made for them to sleep, a house must be built to keep them warm in the cold times, but first, they must form a "family".

At the first full moon after the arrival of Sana, Schut and the Old Man prepared to create this more formal "family". Schut, as we have said, had a staff, about as tall as a man, with marks cut into it, and items hung from it which were associated with his "lodge", his own "family". When Schut had first taken a wife, he received his staff from the Old Man. At the birth of each of his children, he cut a notch on the staff.

Schut had carved seven notches in his lodge staff. Two were for children born before Ach, but they had both died before Ach could know them. The first died in the depths of winter, when Ach's mother was still quite young, the second of sickness when Ach was less than two summers old. These marks in the staff had a second mark, across them, to indicate that these children no longer took breath.

Two other marks came after Ach, these also bore the second mark, a boy and a girl. The boy had died at birth, about one summer after Schut's second child had died. The other, the one that brought Ach the most sadness, was a sister. She was born when Ach was of about four summers. When she was of four summers, she had an accident. She was playing with some of the other children, climbing the rocks just at the base of the great rock wall behind the village. She had fallen and injured her head. She lingered for almost a moon, but gradually lost her strength. Her wounds were just too bad to heal. She finally took fever, and Schut, for the fourth time, took his lodge staff, and crossed through a child-mark.

Life in the valley could be hard. The Lodge Staffs of some the families bore witness to great sorrow. They were a source of pride for a mother and father, to show the numbers of their children, and keep track of their ages. But they were also a source of great sadness, a constant reminder to all the parents of their main mission in life: to do all they could to secure the lives of their children.

And so, Schut cut and shaped a nice staff for his son. He took it with him to the council fire and presented it to Ach and Sana. When Ach and Schut had saved Schut-Tah from the wild beast, the men had removed the beast's long, curved teeth and given them to Schut-Tah. He had tied one of the teeth to the lodge staff of Schut, to thank his brother, and to show all that his brother had saved his life. Now, as Schut presented the newly cut lodge staff to Ach, Schut-Tah rose and tied the second tooth to it, to remind all that it was Ach's quick thinking, and a handy stone, that had saved his uncle.

Ach's mother's name was Sun-Ti, "bright star". She was named for her beautiful, sparkling eyes. But as she rose to congratulate her son on this important day, those eyes were filled with tears. They were tears of joy for the new man and wife, but also of sadness as she thought about the marks on Schut's lodge staff, and of the marks that might one day be on this new staff, belonging to Ach… the marks of new little ones, and of those who had been lost.

45

- o 0 o -

Building

With the marriage now made formal with the presentation of the lodge staff, the men began to speak about a house for Ach. In the Rock village, most of the lodges had been built in a similar way. This may be because the men usually worked together, and so the hands that built one house, would have helped build many of the others. But also, it's because the building materials were much the same. At the base of the great rock wall behind the village, there were many, many stones that had fallen from the wall over the years. Many of these stones were flat, and of a size that made them easy to move and suitable for the walls of a home.

The usual technique was to first remove any fallen trees or plants that were in the spot where the home would sit. These might be dug out with sticks, or burned away, or both. Then, the men would take sticks and begin to loosen and scrape the dirt. In the area of the village, the dirt would sometimes be as deep as the length of a man's foot. With the dirt removed, there would be a solid place to place the first stone layer. Stones would be selected for this layer that were larger than the upper stones, usually as thick as the length of a man's foot and sometimes quite heavy.

The first heavy stones were placed to be the base of the new walls, and then water would be mixed with some of the loose dirt. Mud made from this dirt will be laid on top of the first stones, just before the second layer was placed, filling in the gaps to keep out the wind. As the layers built up to the level of the outside dirt, a doorway would be marked off. As the layers of stone rose higher, thinner, lighter stones were used, as it was difficult to raise the heavy stones to these higher levels. At the height of a man's chest, openings would be left to let air and light in during the warm times.

The layers would continue, until pieces of wood were cut and laid across the top of the door and the air openings, then the last couple of layers of stone. Usually, one wall would be higher than the others. Wood poles would be cut and would be laid across, from wall to wall, looking on top like steps, rising to the highest wall. Then across these, running down the slope of the roof, would be small sticks, laid side by side, all across the roof. Finally, mud would be placed on top of the small sticks, to harden and keep out the rain and snow. From time to time, the men would add mud on top of a roof, if the rain had started to leak in.

In one corner, under the high side of the roof, a hole would be left, to let smoke escape. On the floor, just under this hole, some thinner, flat stones would be stood on edge. These, plus the corner of the room, would make a place where a fire could be built for cooking and warmth during the cold times. During warm times, the women would make fires and cook outside. A heavy piece of skin was tied to the roof near the smoke hole. In cold times, it could be pulled over to make the smoke hole a little smaller, to help keep the home warmer. In warm times, it could be pulled back, to let more air flow through the house. In cold times, skins would be hung across the door, to keep out the wind and white cover.

When Schut had built his house, he thought ahead to the day when he would build a second lodge for a son. He had built one wall of his house, the highest wall, with no openings, and had made sure that on that side of the house, there would be room one day to add three new walls, and make a second house, using the common wall. This made the building of Ach's house quicker, and easier, and would help keep the family members close together. Just across the path, so the doorways would look toward each other, the men continued their building, a house for Sinc and Ayea.

- o 0 o -

Laughing

And so, from mid-summer, when Sana had been welcomed into the family of the Rock village, the people had been busy. At the council fire, the lodge staff was presented, and the building of a house for Ach and Sana had begun. Now, as the cool air blew up the valley, in time for the turning of the leaves, the lodge was done. Ach and Sana moved out of the house of Schut and Sun-Ti and began to sleep in their new home.

The fall was the time for "laughing". Now, "laughing" doesn't mean a time for jokes and comedy. It's an expression used by the women for the time in the early fall, when the darkness starts to arrive early in the evening, and the first breath of cool air drifts up the valley. It is a time when giggling and quiet laughter can be heard when one walks through the village after dark. It is a time for men and wives to be together. It is a time of leisure, when much of the work of preparing for the cold time is done. It is a time for relaxing. The women say "when laughter comes with the cool air, babies come at mid-Summer".

Mid-summer is a good time for babies to arrive. Food is most plentiful in the village, and the health of the women is likely to be at its best. A woman can eat well in the early summer, and gain weight. This fat helps to preserve her health when a nursing baby's demands increase.

When babies are born at this time, the other women help with the mother's work and the storing of food for the winter. Extra food must be ready for her, because the baby will be half a year old at mid-Winter. The growing baby puts quite a strain on the mother's health, demanding much milk at this time. Toward the end of winter, as spring is arriving, the baby's demand is quite high, but this is the time when new foods begin to become available as the weather warms, and so the mother can eat well and continue to provide enough milk.

A baby born in early Spring will hit this high-demand time at mid-Winter. This can be a difficult time for the mother if food is not plentiful. A nursing baby who is nearly a year old by Spring demands a lot of milk. Sometimes, if food is not available, the mother will grow quite thin, and perhaps her milk will stop, putting the baby in great danger. The other women will have to act quickly to help it start to eat normal food, or it will be lost. The mother as well will be at risk. If her health is pushed too far at mid-Winter, and if the village cannot find fresh meat, she may be lost as well.

And so, having babies arrive at the best time of year is very important. The "laughing" is really no laughing matter. The women know these things. They are taught by their mothers, and their grand-mothers. The women know they must take care of one another. Each knows that in the next cold time, she could be the one in trouble, the one who needs the help of the others. Knowing this, each makes sure to do her part and always be helpful to her "sisters" in need.

- o 0 o -

Cover

The first fall of the white cover came early that year. The fall had passed, and the village's preparations for the long cold time had gone well. With the new hunting tools that Ach and Sinc had made, the men had hunted well, and the women had put away much dried meat, berries and other food. Having the two new women, Sana and Ayea, in the village meant more mouths to feed. But the girls worked hard and helped prepare much more food that just they would need. It grew cold, but the lodges were warm, the people well fed, and the families faced the coming cold time without fear.

As more and more of the white cover fell, many of the animals began to move down out of the high areas in the valley. It was easier to find food down below, and they could get to water at the stream. In the past, Ach had sometimes seen tracks near an old lodge near the base of the rock wall. The lodge had been built too close to the wall, and falling rocks and ice had damaged it, prompting the builder to find a safer location.

Now, with the heavy cover, Ach again saw the tracks. Hard to make out in the deep white, he suspected it was the fox. Wolves will catch and kill a fox if they can, but the wolves usually did not come near the village. Perhaps the fox felt it was safer here. He could avoid the hungry wolves, and if he kept out of sight, maybe the men wouldn't notice him either. Perhaps he also thought that he might, now and then, find a morsel of food to steal from the men, as there were few rabbits for him to hunt higher up.

One evening, near the long night, Ach walked with Sana down to the stream, to fetch water before it became dark. As they walked, Ach noticed the tracks again, just to the side of the trail, heading down to the water. He continued to watch them as they moved farther off the trail, just a bit further downstream. There he noticed, sitting and looking down the valley again, was the fox. Seeing Ach, the fox turned and quickly headed back to his hiding place under the fallen roof of the old lodge.

Remembering before, the way the fox had seen the Cloud man running, way down in the valley, Ach continued to look downstream. As the light faded, looking tired and cold, he could just make out the sight of someone walking up the trail. It was not a grown person, too small. Ach began to walk in that direction. As he could see the person was weak, he quickened his steps. In the dim light, as fresh white began to fall from the sky, he could make out the face of a very young girl.

Surprised at the sight of her, he could tell she was nearly starved, and very cold. Her face was pale and drawn, but seemed familiar. Then Ach noticed something in her hand. It was a necklace with a small, black arrow point, just like the one Sana wore, just like he had given to Cree. "Ach?", she asked, not sure she recognized him. "Ach," he said, "Ach!" pointing to his chest. Still with summers no more than two hands and two, this small young girl had made it, all the way from her village in the heavy white cover.   She made a three-day walk, all alone, with only quick instructions given to her several moons ago. It would not be the last time Ach would be surprised at her resourcefulness.

The original idea of trading for Cree was mostly based on keeping her from being traded to the men that Schut and the others felt were Coyotes. They said that she would be a second wife for Ach, but they only intended this to become so after two or three more years, when she would be of a better age to leave her mother. But now that Crow Woman had thrown her out, she had come to the Rock village much sooner than anyone had expected.

Cree's entrance into the village would be quite different than that of Sana, just a few months earlier. Instead of the whole village coming out to welcome her, Sana ran ahead to tell Schut and Sun-Ti that Ach was bringing the cold, nearly starved traveler up from the stream. Sun-Ti said that she should stay in the lodge of Schut for now, since she was so young, and since Ach and Sana had just moved into their own lodge. Instead of being a wife, Cree would be welcomed, later when she had regained her strength, as a new daughter for Schut and Sun-Ti.

The young girl was quite confused by all of this. She was nervous. After all that she had been through, she was quite afraid that the Rock people would not accept her. But Sun-Ti soon put her at ease. She was welcomed into the lodge with a mother's touch. She was fed, and bedded down with the younger sister and brother of Ach. When she recovered her strength, she remained on edge for some time, always being quick to help with chores, to be seen working hard and to make sure others thought she was useful. It would be some time before she would feel fully a part of the Rock family.

-o0o-

New Tools

When Coyotes came into the valley, and were caught by the village men, they were killed. Their bodies, weapons and all possessions were buried, swept away. All would deny seeing them, to help prevent future attacks from their tribes. But when the Raiders had been defeated, with men killed numbering two hands and four, the Old Man said this "wiping away" would not be done.

First, the task of hiding the bodies of so many men would be difficult, and there was other work to be done then. But also, the Old Man sensed that it would be best for neighboring tribes to know that the group of raiders had been defeated. Perhaps it would give heart to other small villages, attacked by such evil men. And perhaps, it would make such men think better about raiding.

The Old Man had told the others to drag the dead raiders down the valley. There a small hill stuck out from the ridge, covered with old, windswept trees. The birds that eat death roosted in those trees. Many of the huge black birds could be seen, wings spread out like the arms of a man, sunning themselves. The bodies were placed at the base of the hill where the birds could feast on them. With much to eat, the nests of the birds would soon be full of young. The Old Man liked the idea of the scary birds guarding the entrance to their valley. Perhaps future coyotes or raiders would see them as a bad omen, and go elsewhere.

So the Rock and Cloud men gathered together the weapons dropped by the dying men. They looked among the skins the raiders had worn for anything that might be useful to the villages. They checked the pouches of the raiders for tools, weapons, anything of value to the tribes. If an item was found that was not understood, the Old Man said "do not throw it aside, we will think about it, and try to know its use." He knew this was an opportunity for the village people to see much that others owned and used, in the same way much could be learned by meeting the traders and the people of other villages.

Cree had recognized one of the items. It was a stone that was flat and round and about as big as the palm of a woman's hand. The stone was mostly circular, but had a "corner" that was long, thin, and quite sharp. Cree showed Sinc how to hold it, and how to use it to make holes in skins and other objects. It was a type of holing tool that she had seen used in the village of her uncle. Sinc then made a few others like it, and Cree began teaching the other women how to make holes, cut thin strings, and fit skins together in a way that kept a person quite warm.

Ach and Sinc looked at the weapons of the men, and saw something they did not understand. They looked at and handled the spears and arrows of the raiders, which were much like the ones already used by Rock people. But two other items were unusual. One was a short, lighter spear, heavier than an arrow, but lighter than a normal spear. The other was a stick, a little longer than a man's forearm. The stick had an unusual notch on one end, and this is what puzzled the boys. Three of the raiders had such tools, so these were not just simple sticks. These sticks were made to do something special. But what? Ach and Sinc would talk with the Old Man about them.

The Old Man listened to the boys. As they spoke, Sinc noticed that the ends of the light spears looked like they would fit into the end of the short sticks. "Could they be used together?", he asked. The Old Man thought about this. He said that he had heard stories, about men who lived far toward the rising sun. Where they lived, there were no mountains, only flat ground, no trees to hide a hunter, only grass. He wondered if these two tools could be used together, perhaps to throw the short spear farther than a man could throw a normal spear. If it was true, maybe this would help the men of the flat country to throw farther, so they did not have to get so close to their prey. He asked the boys to try it, and see what happened.

Quietly, the old man took the walking staff of the dead leader of the raiders. He cut deep notches in it. One for each of the dead men, they numbered two hands and four. He took necklaces and some other items from the dead men and tied them to the staff, like those used by the Rock families. In difficult times, he would find this staff, and show it to the Rock people again, to remind them of their strength, their bravery, and their fighting as one alongside the Cloud people. Several times, when things looked bad for the village, this staff, and the Old Man, would give them the courage to go on.

-o0o-

The Place of Waiting

As the cold time came to an end, and the weather began to warm, ice would melt by day, and then become hard again in the cold night. This changing between water and ice sometimes made rocks loosen and fall from the great rock wall. Sometimes, this would damage The Place of Waiting.

At the end of the rock wall, a short walk from the village, there was a place where the edge of the great rock stood out a bit from the rest of the valley wall. Tucked back into the corner, back in behind the great rock, was a space. The place was not too wide, perhaps the height of two men at the front, getting more narrow as it went back. It was quite high however, like a large crack between very tall rocks. The bottom part was filled with rocks and rubble that had, over a very long time, fallen from above. High overhead, the rocks came back together, and so formed a roof and high ceiling, maybe the height of a hand and three or four men.

Long ago, before the Old Man was born, the elders had chosen this place. They had taken rocks from the floor of the space and made a high stone wall across the entrance. They built a doorway in the wall, so the lost ones might be carried inside, to wait. The doorway was up, much higher than the height of a man. The elders had taken two long lodge poles, and carved them so that smaller posts would fit between, as steps. This structure was lifted up and leaned against the doorway when the Rock people needed to enter. It was lowered to the ground when they left, so that animals could not climb into the room.

This was The Place of Waiting, a place where the lost ones would wait to cross over, into the next world. Inside the doorway, there was a floor, made of wood poles, crossing the space. The Old Man told a story of a time long ago, when the men of the Rock village had built this floor. The place of waiting had already been used for many, many years by that time. The bodies of the old ones, the children, the women and the men who had gone, had filled the place until it was difficult to place others inside.

And so the men, the Old Man's grand-father, and great-grand-father had built this floor. The floor was above the waiting place of the oldest ones. From that time on, the lost ones would be placed above the floor. The Old Man had shown Ach a hole, near the entrance to the place, where he could look down, into the lower room. There he saw many. It saddened Ach to see the bodies of so many small ones. The Old Man told Ach to greet them, to speak with respect, to apologize for disturbing them.

Above the floor were the bodies of the more recently lost. More recent meaning, they had gone since the Old Man was a very young child. There were many in this space also. Some poles had been placed across the space, up above the floor, two or three poles wide, enough to make a comfortable place to sit. There, several of the lost, mostly adults, had been placed in a sitting position, quietly waiting. Sometimes, the bodies of the tiny ones were laid in the laps of the adults, who would look after them.

This day, the Old Man brought Ach and Sinc to see the place. They offered their respects, and their apologies for this intrusion, and then they entered the place to look and see if damage had been done by ice or falling rocks. But this time, there was not much to be repaired. The rock wall the men had built long ago stood firm, safe in its place, mostly protected from rock and ice by the rocks high above. The men cleaned away a few leaves and fallen branches. They sang their song of the lost ones, bid them good journey, and left them to wait, in the peace and quiet of the rock wall.

"Ach," said the Old Man, "you know the place of my old woman. When my time comes, place me there, next to her. And if small ones are lost, place them in my lap, and I will look after them. Tell their mothers, they will not be alone." Ach said nothing, placing his hand on the Old Man's shoulder. He couldn't imagine life without this man, a member of the village whose true age no one remembered. He had always advised the tribe, spoken strength to them, and guided them in times of trouble. But as they stood there, Ach knew that one day he would face life without the Old Man beside him. Ach resolved that when that day came, he must be ready.

- o 0 o -

Spirit Woman

The first time it had happened, the Old man was frightened. Perhaps because it was a long, long time ago, when the "Old Man" was only a boy of three or four summers. He had been walking the path alongside the water, behind his mother and the other women. As a boy, as should be expected, his attention was usually far from the women. He threw rocks into the water, and looked around at everything…everything except where he was going. This time, he noticed the quiet. Quiet is nice, except that this time, it meant that he had fallen rather far behind the women.

Looking around, and calling out, he realized that no one could hear him. The women had walked on, along the stream, and now the "Old Man" was alone. His heart started to pound as the fear rose up inside him. Was he "lost"? Would they find him again? Would he be in trouble? As the fear boiled up, and his eyes began to fill with tears, he turned, and he saw her. She was an old woman, but strange. Not a Rock woman, nor a Cloud, she was different. Different, yet somehow, very familiar. He had never seen her before, but she seemed close, like family, like a grandmother.

He looked at her and his fear evaporated. "Before you lead, you must learn to follow", she said. Her voice was warm, comforting. She pointed to a rock, and the "Old Man" sat down, and rested. He noticed that her clothes were different, not the same as the skins worn by his mother and the others. He asked her where she had come from and she turned and pointed to a place at the base of the great rock wall.

In a few moments, through the silence, the "Old Man" heard familiar voices. It was his mother and her sister, calling to him as they quickly searched. They feared that he had fallen into the water, or that a snake or other animal had found him. They were afraid, and so their voices became angry when they saw him. That is the way with mothers, the quickest way to anger them, is to frighten them.

They saw him sitting all alone, on a rock, in the shade of a great tree looking not upset, not afraid, but quite relaxed. He didn't even seem to be worried that they would punish him. They asked where he had been. "With the lady", he said. "What lady?", they asked, believing that there were no other women around. He turned to look for her, but she was gone. "Where did she come from?", they asked. He pointed to the place at the base of the rock wall.

They looked at each other. At only three or four summers old, he had never been to the Place of Waiting. He did not know its purpose. "What did she say?", they asked. "She said that before I lead, I must learn to follow". This seemed very strange to the women. And then he said "I am sorry that I fell behind". This apology seemed even stranger and the two women felt that they should leave this place, quickly, and rejoin the other Rock women.

From that day, the "Old Man" understood the role he must play. First, as a child, he followed. He knew that leaders needed followers, followers who paid attention, and did their part, and supported the group. As a growing boy and as a man, he would look for followers who would support him. And with their support, he would one day lead the Rock people.

He had again seen the woman from time to time throughout his long life. When trouble was near, he would sometimes see her over his shoulder. The others did not know she was there, but her presence calmed the Old Man, and took away his fear. He had seen her at the council fire the night before the Raiders were defeated. The strength of her face, her calm, let him know that his plan would be successful. At these times, she gave him the confidence that he would then give to the people. He believed that she lived at the Place of Waiting, and that one day, on his last day, he would see her one final time.

- o 0 o -

Praise

From Schut and Schut-Tah, the Old Man felt loyalty. When he stood at the council fire and talked of what the village needed to do, he knew that Schut and Schut-Tah would stand with him, would follow him, and in so doing, this would help hold the village together. The Rock men followed the Old Man because they trusted him. They knew the value of his wisdom, the strength of his experience, and the fairness of his word.

From Ach and from Sinc, the old man felt almost a kind of reverence. They were young, and inexperienced, and they stood in awe of all that the Old Man knew. They consulted him on many things, and because he valued the strength of their minds, he not only spoke to them, but asked them what they thought, how they would solve a problem. This was good teaching for them. It would make them value and respect others. One day, it would make them leaders.

But from the girls, the Old Man felt something different. Sana, Ayea and Cree had come from places outside the village. When they arrived, they had to find ways to fit themselves into the "family" that was the village. The others had done well in greeting them, and making them feel that they belonged, but still, they lacked true family in the village. But in their working, they often helped take care of the Old Man. His woman had gone, in the cold time, several seasons ago, and so he was alone.

And so the Old Man saw something in the girls. He saw that they needed true family in the same way that he sometimes felt that he did. His own two daughters had taken husbands in other villages many summers ago. His two sons had both been lost, one to sickness, and one to an injury suffered while hunting. As the girls prepared him food, and mended the skins he wore, he came to look at them as his family.

One day, at the council fire, when the Rock and Cloud people were gathered around, the Old Man stood to speak. The group quieted, to show respect for this well-known leader, a man who served, unofficially, as "great-grandfather" to many of them. The Old Man said, "Many times, our villages speak, of the bravery of our men. Many times their strength, and the hunting skills that keep us fed, warm, and safe, are praised at the council fire, in front of all the people. But it is not so often, that we speak of the strength…of our women."

He pointed to one of the Cloud women, and asked her to stand. As she did, he said "This woman has brought us a hand and four children! Her four sons and five daughters are strong members, of our villages. She has much to be proud of, and we should all be proud of her". The woman's face turned red as all looked at her. Several of the adults in the group shouted, "yes!", and "strong woman!" as she sat down, and scurried to hide her face.

He then pointed to the wife of The Wolf, and to the wife of Schut, and asked them to stand. "These women hold our groups together". "Since each one has a daughter who has taken a husband in the other village, both are happy to have their daughters so close to them. Each knows that the other woman will look after her daughter and be a second mother to her. Every day, these women teach their skills to our young women, showing them the many things they must know, to keep our villages healthy and strong".

He then asked Sana, Ayea and Cree to stand. *"My girls'"*, he called them, for the first time. "They each came to our villages from outside. They came here alone, hoping to be accepted. But even though our people are not their true family, the hands of these girls are always busy helping to feed us, helping to fit warm skins for us, helping hold our families together. These three are smart women. They brought new skills to us from their home villages, and they teach those skills to all of us"

The girls, who were standing near the Old Man stepped toward him. All together, they put their arms around him and together gave him a big hug. This kind of embrace was not something the Old Man was used to, and they giggled to see that now, his face was red. The people all shouted their approval. The women, the girls, and even the Old Man, all dried their eyes. With the council fire now burned down, the men began to light torches for the walk home.

Before the group dispersed, the Wolf stood to speak. "A few days ago, as I was down at the end of the valley, near the river, I saw the Trader. He told me that he wishes to go trading again. This time, he wants to walk down the river, passed where the water is wide and smooth, to the place where the land becomes flat. He says that the Walking Men will make their camp there, three moons after the Long Night. If we wish to join him, he will meet us at the end of the valley". "Let us speak more of this, and we will decide", the Old Man said.

-o 0 o-

Down River

The walk to the end of the valley was already quite long. Most of the men did not travel that far to hunt, only to trade for wives with the other villages. Most of the women never went that far. To turn down river and walk to the place where the water became wide and calm was even farther. Only the Old Man had seen that water before. To go passed it, and down onto the flat land was farther that anyone in the Rock or Cloud villages had ever traveled.

But times for the Rock and Cloud villages were good. Again, they had come through the cold times well. Food was plentiful, the people were fed and healthy, and the villages had many things to trade. In addition, the Old Man could see that several items taken from the fallen Raiders had become useful tools for the Rock people. He knew that seeing and trading with new people sometimes held the promise of new ideas, new techniques, new ways of surviving.

"We will go", he said. By now, Ach and Sinc had made several more of the throwing sticks and short spears. The Old Man asked them to bring those, and several of the long spears that they had been making. Sinc gathered several good spear points, his holing tools, and a few skins that Cree had helped make. They fit snugly around a man's chest and shoulders and when larger skins were worn over them, a man could keep warm, even in very cold weather. The others gathered skins, dried grapes, dried meat and other items, and prepared for the long journey.

The Old Man woke the group early. The Cloud men had come over to the Rock village the night before, and slept outside, near the lodges. There was usually grumbling when the Old Man woke the men to leave early for hunting, but this morning the whole group woke with excitement at the idea of such a long journey, of seeing things not seen before.

Several of the Cloud Men and boys stood with the Rock men and boys, and said goodbye to the women. The Old Man told them to watch out for themselves while the men were gone, and to hide themselves if trouble was spotted. The group of men, numbering three hands, turned and headed off down the valley in the still dark morning. At the end of the day, the group reached the place near the river where they had met the trader before. They saw his fire as the sky was growing dark.

Sleeping the night on large elk skins, they rose again before the sun, rolled up their skins and began to walk, again with excitement quickening their pace. As they walked, they ate the dried meat and dried fruit that the women had packed for them. As the afternoon approached, the Trader told the boys that finding fresh meat would be a good idea, since he was not sure what they would see when they reached the flat ground. They made their camp in the late afternoon and the boys scampered off to see what rabbits, fish or other foods they could find.

At the end of the third long day, the group could see the fires of a small village on the edge of the water, near the place where the water began to grow wider and still. The Trader called out while the men were still some distance from the village, so the people would not be surprised by the group. "Woooooooeeeee", he called, hands held near his mouth. "Woooooooeeeee" he called again.

As the group watched, several men stepped into view near the village, and a few others, quite near the group. The village had been watching the approaching men and had taken up their weapons, until they knew the intent of the visitors. The Trader raised his hands, empty and open, as did several of the other men. One of the village men raised his hand in response. "Make a long line, with some distance between each man. Follow me, one by one down the trail. They will see that we mean them no harm", the Trader advised.

While sharing food, the men talked and signed with the men of the Lake Village. After explaining that the group was traveling to trade with the men on the flat ground, some of the village men signed that they would like to join the group. The Trader stood and signed his pleasure at this. He signed that the group would leave again before the sun rose, and the men began to spread out skins for the night.

-o0o-

The Flat

The group walked on, now for a fourth long day. As they traveled, the Rock and Cloud men talked and signed with the men of the Lake Village. They could tell that, even though their words were similar, their lives were somewhat different. The Lake men found ways to catch fish along the shores, in places stacking rocks in the shallow water as a way of trapping the fish, making them easier to catch. The animals that the lake people hunted were mostly the same, but because their mountains were not as high, they did not see the same goats and elk that the Rock and Cloud men hunted. None knew of course, how different they would find the Walking Men to be.

As the day wore on, the men noticed that the mountains were fading behind them. As they passed the rocks at the end of the lake, where the water fell down and became a river again, all that remained were rolling hills. The trees were fading as well as the land opened up into grass covered slopes with occasional brush. As the afternoon grew late and the sun sank lower behind them, the Trader looked around for the last high point before the hills faded completely away. He asked the boys to hurry up the hill and look well off to where the sun would rise. The sun, now low behind them, would make smoke out on the horizon easier to see. He told the boys to mark the direction if they saw any.

While the boys rushed up the hill, the men looked around for brush and wood to make a fire. The Trader said that if the Walking Men were out there on the flat, where he thought they made their camp at this time of year, a fire could be built that the Walking Men might see. They would build it on top of the hill, just after the night sky became dark. From on top of the hill, the boys called to the men, and pointed out to the flat, way out to the horizon. They could see the smoke of the Walking Men.

The men carried wood and brush high up the hill and made a pile. When it grew fully dark, they lit the fire and fed it fuel to make it as bright as they could. They would not know if the Walking Men were watching. They would not know if the Walking Men would be interested to trade. And though the Trader had not said so, he was just a little bit nervous, about whether the Walking Men would be friendly. As the fire died down, the group ate some of their dried meat, grapes and berries. They spread their skins again and tried to rest, but the excitement made sleep difficult.

At dawn, the men rose, rolled up their skins and followed the river out onto the flat in the direction that the boys had marked. They had no intention of walking all the way to the camp of the Walking Men. Not only was it far out on the flat and would be difficult to find over such a great distance, but they surely didn't want the Walking Men to fear them, and to attack. They walked until the sun was high in the sky then gathered some grass and brush to make a smoky fire. As the smoke rose into the light breeze, they spread out their skins and waited.

- o 0 o –

Walking Men

Mid-morning, the boys came running to the Trader. Out on the flat, under the still rising sun, the group could see two, or maybe three hands of men, walking toward them. The Trader, as he had done at the Lake village, stood up, and held his hands up, empty and open. To his relief, one of the men walking toward them did the same, and must have called for the others near him to do so as well. The Rock and Cloud men joined this ritual as the two groups signed that each intended the other no harm.

As the men approached, the group could see that one man had long white hair, blowing in the light breeze. He looked to be the oldest, so they too it seemed, had an "Old Man." He came forward, with a couple of young boys, and two or three other grown men. About two hands of men stayed back, away from the group, as if to say that if things did not go well, they would be there to help the white-haired one. As the Walking Men grew near, with the gentle breeze blowing from behind them, Ach and Sinc noticed something funny. It was a smell, the smell of animals.

Living out on the flat was a very different life than what Ach and the others were used to. The flat was a dry place, flat and endless. These people followed large herds of animals, in order to hunt them. They moved from place to place, camping where they knew they would find water. The Trader explained that these people moved across the flat in a regular way, worked out over many summers, to find water in the warm times, to find animals to hunt, and to find shelter for the cold times. He had known that the Walking Men made their camp near this river on the third full moon after the Long Night.

Killing and butchering the large animals that the Walking Men hunted was a big effort. It required the whole group's help to skin, cut, carry and dry the meat. This effort left all the group's members covered in the animal's blood, and the smell of their entrails. Far out on the flat, there was no wood for cooking fires.   The Walking Men gathered the dried droppings of the large animals as fuel. All these things combined to provide the Walking Men with a unique, and powerful, smell.

As the weather warmed, the Walking Men would follow the animals up the flat, toward the Standing Star, the star that did not move, but held its place all year in the night sky. At the Long Day, they would turn, and move for several days toward the place where the sun rises. They would then turn away from the Standing Star, following the animals as the animals followed the grass. As the weather began to grow cold, the Walking Men would walk far down the flat, to the place where they camped during the cold times. The place was protected from the winds by high cliffs and their dried meat would feed them until the grass began growing again. As the weather would again start warming, they moved out once more, along their endless path.

The white-haired one sat at the edge of the skins. His words were quite different, so if he was to be understood, it would be through signing. The Old Man moved up, just opposite him. The Old Man pointed to Schut and Schut-tah and to the Wolf, and tried to introduce them. The white-haired one pointed to himself, and held out a bit of his hair, as if to say that was his name. Then "White-Hair" held up his strong-hand, and said a word, then pointed to the man sitting next to him and said the same word, holding out his strong hand, as if this man was White-Hair's close family member, his "strong hand".

- o 0 o -

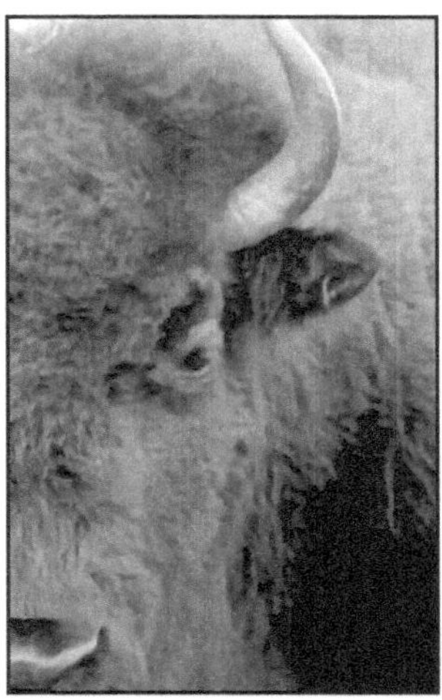

Business

Both groups began to lay out things that might be traded. The Old Man motioned for White-Hair and Strong Hand to come, to look, and examine the items. Strong Hand called for the boys with him to bring forward several skins, strange, large skins like no one in the group had ever seen.

At one point, White-Hair took some of his dried meat, and using the edge of his spear point, began to cut at it, to get a piece that would fit into the mouth. This looked a little clumsy, and so Sinc held up his hand. He crawled out across the skins, cautiously, and showed White-Hair a stone tool he had made. He showed the man how to hold it, and demonstrated cutting the meat more easily, since the sharp stone was rounded on the back, so not to cut the hand.

White Hair liked the tool, and after trying it, attempted to hand it back to Sinc. But Sinc, waved his hand, then put both hands together, palms up and empty, and made a motion as if he were giving the tool to White-Hair. This pleased White-Hair and he called for one of his boys to come forward. He carried a skin that looked smaller than the largest skins, but even so was still almost as big as a bull elk skin. This one was soft and fresh and looked of good quality.

The boy handed it to Sinc, and White-Hair signed "trade", and looked at Sinc to see if it was accepted. Sinc smiled and nodded. That bit of business was done. Sinc was learning the trading business well.

The Rock and Cloud men all looked at the skin and nodded their approval. They touched Sinc on his shoulders and waved their hands to White-Hair. This meeting of very different peoples was beginning in a positive way. The trading continued, with elk and rabbit skins and other stone and bone tools. The men shared food, the Rock and Cloud men ate the meat from the animals of the Walking Men. The Walking Men tasted the dried berries, the dried grapes and the elk meat that the Rock and Cloud men had brought.

As the sun was moving lower, Ach let it show on his face that he was puzzled. He had Sinc stand up, and draped an elk skin over him, to show the Walking Men the size of the animal. But then, with his still puzzled face, he motioned to the huge skins spread before him, and asked about them. White-Hair stood and called to several of his men. Three of them got under one of the largest skins, holding their hands high, and still just barely got the leg-skin of the huge beast off the ground. Strong Hand put his hands, with pointed fingers, near his head, and made strange sounds as his feet struck the ground and kicked dust up into the air.

The Rock men stared wide eyed, not really understanding, but at least knowing that these huge skins came from huge animals, animals that looked quite dangerous. Sinc then stood, again very cautiously, and picked up one of the spears of the Walking Men. He held it near the men still holding up the skin, as if to ask how the Walking Men attacked such a large animal. White-Hair and Strong Hand stood together and held their spears. At first they made motions like they threw their spears, and after making that motion several times, they finally held their spears tight and in a mock way, thrust them at the animal's heart.

Sinc then motioned to the men to put down the skin and he asked Ach to move the smaller skin further away from the group, a distance equal to the distance Sinc and Ach had been practicing with the spear-throwing sticks, left by the Raiders. Sinc motioned for the men to step back, which White-Hair and Strong Hand did with keen interest. Sinc picked up three of his smaller throwing spears and quickly threw them, one, two, three, each one hitting the skin.

With that, Ach picked up one of the long spears and rushed toward the skin in a mock attack. The Walking Men's mouths dropped open. Sinc had just thrown three spears, farther than they had ever seen a spear thrown, with each one hitting the skin. Ach had attacked with a long spear in a way that would help the Walking Men avoid the anger of a wounded beast. These new weapons were of <u>great</u> interest to them.

- o 0 o -

Serious Business

White-Hair, excited, invited all to sit back down at the skins. He called to his boys and to the men sitting back behind, and sent them running off to toward their camp. He then offered more meat, some cooked roots, water and other comfort to the traders. After they had eaten, they talked and signed all they could sign. As the light of the fire finally died down, they all lay down on the skins to sleep.

As the sun rose in the morning, the traders realized that the group of Walking Men had grown. After walking what must have been all night, the boys had returned with several other men, carrying animal skins, several of them, in all sizes. With them came several women and young girls. The women carried water in bags made from the large animal's organs. The girls carried bone tools, polished bones, and bones that looked like they might be from large birds, hollow, tied into necklaces.

When the traders were awake, White-Hair again motioned for the traders to come and sit at the edges of the skins. He could see that Ach and Sinc had brought with them four of the long spears. He could also see two throwing sticks, and two hands of the shorter spears. White-Hair motioned to Sinc, in a smiling way, to put the spears and throwing sticks out on the trading skins. He was most pleased when Sinc agreed to do so, and began to call up boys with additional large skins. They also put down several soft, fresh skins of what must have been young animals, even though to the Rock men, they still seemed quite large.

When Ach laid the long spears across the skins, Strong Hand came forward with two nice young girls, each carrying water skins and bone beads. To the surprise of the Rock men, Strong Hand instructed the girls to stay on the skins, apparently they would be part of the deal. The Old Man took four more spear points and a pouch of dried grapes and placed them on the skins. He stood and asked if all agreed. The men, on both sides of the skins, walked around and made serious faces, as if heavily considering the value of the deal to each side (as men always do at such sessions).

White-Hair stood and spoke to his people, making sure they were all in agreement. When the talking seemed to be done, he turned to the Old Man and signed "Trade". The Old Man looked at his people, and with their agreement, signed the same. The deal was done. It was the largest single swap the Trader had ever seen. All seemed to be happy, with the possible exception of the two young girls, who now realized that they would no longer walk with the Walking Men. Their mothers came forward to hug them good bye and the two groups began to gather up their new possessions.

The load of the Rock and Cloud men was so large that White-Hair could see that they could not carry it all. He called to four of his young men and motioned for them to journey to the Rock village, to help carry the items. He signed to them that on their return, the Walking Men would be gone and that they should walk on a line toward the Standing Star to find them again. "Look for our smoke as the sun rises", he told them.

As the two groups parted, each thought about what they had gained. The Rock and Cloud men had several large skins of a kind that people in their valley had never seen, skins that would keep a family warm, even in the coldest of times. They decided that the girls would go one to the Rock village, and one to the Cloud village. Both villages had young men who would be interested in taking wives, and hopefully the smell of the large animals on these two would fade in the mountain air. The girls also came with a skill at making beads and stone tools, which could be used in future trading missions.

The Walking Men felt themselves very lucky. With the short spears and throwing sticks, they would be able to reach animals that before would have gotten away. With the long spears, they could increase the distance between their hunters and the serious injuries or death that may come with a large, wounded animal. And to top it off, White-Hair had a cutting tool that would make it unnecessary to use his bloodied spear point to cut his meat when he ate.

On the way back to the valley, as the men came to the Lake Village, Ach and Sinc traded some of their skins for more spear shafts, this time looking not only for the normal and long shafts, but also for the stick-throwing spear shafts. All the way home they reminded each other of their high skill at trading, and imagined what future missions might hold.

-o0o-

Ash-Ká

An "ash-ká" was a bug. Not a nasty bug, but a cute bug. It was very small, and round, and could fly. It didn't bite, and its shiny round body, with its orange color and tiny black spots, was pretty. The people thought of them as good luck, when they landed on hands or arms, and particularly good luck if they landed on noses. One had landed on tiny Ash-Ká's nose when she was still in her mother's arms, and so it became her name.

The Old Man had taught Ash-Ká that good luck was a good thing, but that many times, luck did no good, if a person wasn't ready for it. One must pay attention, watch for danger, look carefully for food, place feet carefully on trails. Then, when a rock slipped without causing a fall, or a dangerous animal was avoided, we could smile and call it luck if we wanted to, but we should never be careless and just hope luck would take care of us.

Ash-Ká's summers numbered only a hand and three. One day, while the men were off trading with the Walking Men, she was walking with the women in the forest. She was helping with the smallest children as the women looked about, gathering berries and roots. When there were no "human" animals in the valley, no human dangers, the women would sometimes walk quite far down the valley, looking for the best sources of berries or wild grapes.

Then, one of the women heard something that made her uneasy. It was the birds. She had heard them singing shortly before, but now they were "talking". It was as if the birds had seen something, and perhaps been fussing at it, but now they didn't see it. It was as if the birds were asking each other where it went. "Little Ones up!", she shouted, fearing that the birds might have seen something dangerous. "Little Ones up!", the other women and girls repeated, as they rushed to pick up all the babies and youngest children.

Ash-Ká, at such a young age, was certainly not yet the size of the women and older girls. But there, near her, was a "little one", a boy of about two summers. His mother had gathered food and had moved some distance away, carrying her load. Ash-Ká knew that for certain dangers, it was important to get all the Little Ones up off the ground, and into the protective arms of mothers. Since the little boy's mom was farther away, Ash-Ká didn't hesitate, she scooped him up and plopped him onto her hip like a seasoned mother would do.

The name for a fox was Shin-te. Shin-te were never a danger to the Rock people. Shin-te ate rabbits, small birds when they could catch them, and the small squirrels and mice they would chase along the ground. Shin-Tah-ney was the name for a wolf. Wolves were of course dangerous. They could be so even for a grown man, if he were alone, and if the wolves were hungry, as in the cold times. But in the valley, even some distance from the villages, Shin-Tah-ney usually were not seen. They had respect for the men, but they also knew that the men were hunting the same game they would, and so it made no sense to hunt the same ground.

But there was one more member of this "family", Shin-Ta-Nah-hay, the coyote. This was not the human "Coyote", who came to steal the women and young girls. This was the animal that looked bigger than Shin-te, but not quite as large as the Shin-Tah-ney. And instead of hunting in a group, as the Shin-Tah-ney did, the Shin-Ta-Nah-hay was secretive, silent. It would peer from a hiding place until its prey was facing away, then rushing, jumping, taking the prey and disappearing again. This is what made the Shin-Ta-Nah-hay so dangerous to small children.

The Old Man had been coaching Ash-Ká about these dangers. He told her of the Shin-Ta-Nah-hay way of rushing up from behind. He told her that if she were alone and Shin-Ta-Nah-hay was near, she should turn herself around, and look behind, and turn again, and then again, watching in all directions, so the coyote would be confused, and not know from which direction to attack. He told her to put her back to a tree or a large rock, and take stones, or sticks, anything into her hands, to throw if the animal came close.

He told her to make an angry face, and to shout and talk loudly, so the coyote would go away.

He had also told her that if she was with other women and the call came out to watch, she should stand next to a larger woman, stand close, touching, hip to hip, or in her small case, hip to knee. Instead of both of them facing front, as they stood together, she should be turned, facing to the rear. With their eyes covering both front and back, if Shin-Ta-Nah-hay circled around behind them, he would see eyes facing that way too, and be confused.

All the things the Old Man had taught her raced through Ash-Ká's mind as the women called "Little Ones up!". She scooped up the boy and quickly moved next to one of the women, facing to the rear. The woman jumped when Ash-Ká shouted "Not today Shin-Ta-Nah-hay!, Not me, and not this boy!" She caught her breath, "Go away Shin-Ta-Nah-hay!" The other women looked at her, surprised at the angry face and defiant voice of this small girl. They laughed, but they also started to talk loudly, and themselves tell the coyote to go away.

In a few moments, the women heard the birds again, fussing at something, farther down the slope from them. As the fussing sound moved slowly away, the women knew that the coyote was moving away too. He wanted to take one of the Little Ones, but the women's ear for the birds, and the angry face of little Ash-Ká, the Lucky One, had denied him. "Lucky?", Ash-Ká thought, as she saw the smile of the Old Man in her mind. "No", she thought, "not lucky… *Ready!*"

- o 0 o -

Thunder

After several days of walking, the large group consisting of the Rock men, the Cloud men, the Trader, the two girls taken in trade and the four young Walking Men helping carry the many skins, finally arrived at the end of the Rock valley. As they prepared to make camp for the final time before reaching home, the Old Man signed to the four young Walking Men that it would not be necessary for them to go all the way to the Rock village. The Rock and Cloud men, plus the two girls, could carry most of the skins. What remained could be left at the campsite, and Ach and Sinc could return for them. He thanked them for their help and suggested they could head back to the Flat at dawn.

As the sun was rising, the group awoke and ate trail food for the last time. They prepared to say goodbye to the Walking Men, and before parting, showed the boys the path to the Rock village, and pointed way up the valley to the high rock wall. They thanked them for their help and signed that if they traveled this way again, they would be welcome in the Rock and Cloud villages. Ach and Sinc placed the items they could not carry in the trees near the camp site, then picked up their burdens and headed up the valley trail with the other Rock and Cloud men. They would see home before the sun set that day.

The four Walking Men headed back down river. They took with them dried meat and berries the Rock men had given them for the trail. They reached the Lake Village without nervousness, because the Old Man had introduced them to the Lake men a few nights before, and told them the boys would be returning that way. They took water and rested at the Lake Village, and rose early again the next morning, to head for the Flat. They finally reached the edge of the Flat that evening and again prepared to sleep near the river. As they did so, they noticed a large storm gathering out over the Flat, far away, in the direction they intended to travel.

Rising early again, they headed to the place where the Walking Men had been camped at the time of the Trading. The camp was empty, as White-Hair told them it would be, so they prepared to camp once more in the same spot. This time, they noticed that the ground was quite wet. The rains meant life on these dry, dusty plains. The rains meant grass, and the grass was the food that the large animals followed. Usually, the wet ground and the quickly greening grass was a good sign, a sign of life. Usually.

This time would be different. As the young men finally neared the place White-Hair told them the group would be, they did not understand what they were seeing. As far as their eyes could see, in every direction, the soil of the plain was cut and muddied. They realized that the impressions in the mud were from the feet of the large animals, but these were not clean tracks. They were not the even pattern left when a large group grazes side by side in their huge numbers. These were the marks of running animals.

During the storm, heavy thunder had broken across the featureless plain. With no place to take shelter to avoid the lightning, striking all around them, the animals panicked. In their huge numbers, in the black, starless night, they ran, into and over each other in the confusion and the darkness. Unfortunately, the Walking Men's camp was in their path. The Walking Men saw the lightning, heard the booming thunder, and then heard a roar that struck fear in their hearts. It was a constant, screaming bellow and the thunder of many, many hooves. They could feel the pounding of feet on the prairie, feet numbering more than the stars in the sky.

The four young Walking Men finally located the spot that had been the camp. The footprints of the animals covered every bit of ground. No place was spared, and some places were trampled many, many times. The shelters of the Walking Men were pressed into the mud. Most of the bodies were unrecognizable, beaten, muddied, bloodied, into the ground. Silence filled the air. High above, the sky was filled with the birds that eat death, as they prepared to feast on the bodies of the Walking Men, and the many animals that died in the stampede.

The four young men were silent, not wanting to believe what their eyes now told them had happened. They ran around the village, looking for relatives, looking for anyone they recognized, hoping to find someone still alive. There, all alone, near the center of what had been the camp, they found a small boy. He was perhaps one summer old, sitting, covered with mud, crying softly. How had he been spared? Who were his parents? There were several young boys in the group of about that age, but which one was this one? Then, off to the side, hiding behind the body of one of the dead animals, was a young girl, with summers of two hands and two.

Bloody, muddy, she lay tightly against the body of the animal. "There were so many," she said. "They came and came," she stared straight ahead, "it was dawn when they finally stopped running. They jumped over me, stepped on me...", her voice trailed off. Her arm was clearly broken, but fortunately, the bone was not exposed, she would heal. Somehow, by some miracle, the little boy was uninjured. Together, they all sat in the mud, in shock, trying to understand what had happened.

-o0o-

The Trail of the Fox

III

III The Trail of the Fox

The End

The men had returned to the valley after their trading trip. The long walk out to the Flat, to see the Walking Men, had been fruitful. Two young girls had returned with them, and they brought back several of the very large skins from the animals that the Walking Men followed, along with several "smaller" skins from younger animals. In exchange, the Walking Men had some of the long spears, and some of the short spears, thrown with throwing sticks. Both of these new weapons would help the Walking Men stay a bit further away from those very dangerous animals. This would be good for the health of the hunters, and the rest of the tribe as well.

Now, it was time for the Rock men to hunt. Feeling good about the results of the trading trip, the Old Man decided to go with them. Looking for deer, or maybe an elk, the men walked well downstream from the Rock village. They had crossed open ground, and now needed to cross down into a small valley to reach the game trails on the other side. As they descended into the small valley, the trees and brush grew thicker, and thicker. The men joked, quietly, about what they might run into in this thicket. As they reached a part of the trail where visibility through the brush was almost nothing, the Old Man held up his hands.

All stopped. "Ha-Kaa", the Old Man said softly, a bear. The Old Man had smelled it, as the breeze brought the scent up from just below them, down the slope. The men could tell the direction of the breeze, and so could tell the direction of the bear. They moved their weapons into position and began to walk slowly into the brush, hunting the bear. But the Old Man spoke again, "No. OooooWeeee!!!, he shouted. The other men followed quickly, "Hoowww-Ay-Ay." "This brush is too thick, we cannot see", said the Old Man, "better to scare the Bear away, than to have it hunting _us_".

The Old Man laughed as he turned back to the path. "If our smell was as strong as the Walking Men, we never would have smelled that Bear!" But as he turned, he froze in his tracks, his face turned pale as he looked at the tiny bear cub sitting in front of him. His fear was not of the cub of course, but of the mother they had not yet seen. Quickly, he rotated back to the other men, "Schut, Boys, Back Awa…", but he could not finish his warning. All he saw in the faint light, filtering through the trees, was rough brown fur, and the sun glinting off of long, deadly claws.

The blow struck him across his stomach, spinning him around and knocking him to the ground. With spears already well in hand, Schut thrust immediately into the heart of the she-bear, standing now inches away from him. Sinc was next to Schut, and pierced her as well. She dropped, motionless to the ground as a mixture of her blood, and that of the Old Man, covered the path. It took several moments for the group to understand what the Old Man already knew. He was done. If his bleeding slowed, he might last another day, but with his belly sliced open like this, he had no chance.

The men rushed to help him. Ach took a small skin and said they should tie up the Old Man's belly, try to push his insides back where they belonged. Of course, the pain of this was severe, and the Old Man ordered them to stop. "But we will take care of you Old Man!", Schut shouted defiantly, as if the force of his voice would work some magic. "Yes, we will take you back to the village", Ach said. "No", said the Old Man, softly. As the pain raked him, tears filled the eyes of all the hunters. This man who lead the village, who taught the lessons of hunting, of leading, of life, to all the Rock people, was breathing his lasts breaths. To all the people of the village, this loss would be like the loss of a father or grandfather. All would feel the weight of it.

He couldn't walk of course, and even the pain of being carried was too great. So, since he knew he would die anyway, the Old Man said not to move him. "Go, cut up that bear", he said, "she is good meat, a good skin, we must not waste her". All protested. They wanted to get him home, in case the women could help him. But all recognized the Old Man's authority. Although he always invited discussion, never gave orders, this time, the men knew they should be silent, and do as he said.

"Ach, let the others cut her. Come close, talk with me", the Old Man said in a weakening voice. "Ach", he continued, "I have taught you many things. You and Sinc have been the best at learning the lessons, the best at understanding, what a leader must do. You and he must work together, as Schut and Schut-Tah have done, to support each other as you support the tribe".

Tears filled Ach's eyes and fear filled his heart as he thought of the loss of the Old Man. The Old Man could see this panic rising, and said "Ach, you have learned much, but also, I have taught lessons, to many of the others. You must remind them, of the things I have taught them, about hunting, finding food, dealing with outsiders. Together, with you and Sinc, and Schut and Schut-Tah to guide them, the village will survive, the people will do well".

"Ach", he continued, "when we visited the Place of Waiting, I showed you where to put me". "Do you remember?", he asked. "Yes, you showed me the place of your Old Woman, and you pointed to a place next to her", Ach replied, "I remember". "Yes", the Old Man said, almost too softly to hear, "Take me there". Ach's head hung low. He hated this powerless feeling, he hated to give up, but with injuries like these, he knew there was nothing to be done.

As the men gathered up the bear meat and skin, they again lifted the body of the Old Man, and began to walk down the trail. This time, the Old Man felt no pain. His eyes were closed, his faced relaxed and peaceful. On a rock, up the slope from the men, Ach noticed two figures, watching. A woman, a different, unusual looking woman.

With her, a man, standing tall and strong, with dark black hair blowing in the light breeze. The woman's look was comforting, like that of a mother, but Ach did not recognize the man, until a slight smile crept up from one corner of the man's mouth, in a most familiar way. The Old Man raised his hand to Ach, and waved goodbye.

- o 0 o -

Rest

The younger boys on the hunt ran ahead, to tell the village what had happened. Some of the women ran back up the trail, to see if they could help, but to all, it was clear, the Old Man had gone. Schut asked the boys to run to the Cloud village as well, and tell the Wolf. All would gather at the council fire that evening, to talk about what had happened.

By nightfall, the women had prepared the Old Man's body. They had washed away the blood and tied a skin around his middle, to restrain his insides. They braided his long, white hair and readied him to go to the Place of Waiting. Schut went into the Old Man's lodge and found his Lodge Staff. He placed the staff alongside the Old Man, on the poles that would be used to carry him.

At the Council Fire, there was only the sound of the crackling fire, and the quiet weeping of the women. The Wolf stood and spoke to the gathering, which included all the Rock people, and all the Cloud people. "My friends" he said in his confident and reassuring voice, "tonight we are saddened by a great loss, a man who meant something to every one of us. The Old Man was a leader, but he was first, a teacher. His lessons of life have helped each of us, at one time or another. We all mourn him, and we will all miss him. A great sadness will fill our hearts, for many days."

When the Wolf had spoken, Ach rose to address the people. "The Old Man spoke to me this morning, before his eyes closed. He could see that I was frightened by what had happened, and by what might happen, to the Rock people, without him to lead us." Ach also spoke in a strong, confident voice, that of a man, and all the people listened. "He told me not to fear. He reminded me, of the many lessons he had taught, to me, to Schut and Schut-Tah, to Sinc, and to all of us in the village. He could see that I was afraid to be alone, without him, but he told me, that as long as the Rock people work together, and remember the lessons he taught us, our village will survive, and we will do well."

Schut then rose, and stood next to his son. "When Ach helped to save the life of Schut-Tah, Schut-Tah reminded us that a man's strength comes from his father." Schut paused, he looked into the eyes of the people. "This strength comes from the <u>teachings</u> of the father, and of the <u>grand</u>-father", he continued. "This is not the strength of arms and legs, it is the strength of the spirit, of the mind. It is a strength that does not weaken when that father or grand-father is lost. No, this strength stays with us, for all of our days. That is why the Old Man did not fear for us. He knows that we will remember him, remember his teachings. In this way, he will always bring us strength".

"Tomorrow", Schut continued, "we will carry the Old Man to the Place of Waiting. When we do this, we will do so in silence, as we always do when one of us is lost. But tonight, I think the Old Man would prefer, that we speak of him in a way that will ease our sadness, that will help to lift our spirits." As Schut walked around the fire, the faces of all the people followed him. "One thing that I will remember about the Old Man…" as Schut paused, even the fire did not make a noise, "…is that he loved to laugh. He loved to play jokes on us, and to tell stories".

"One day, many years ago, when I was a boy of only a hand or so summers," Schut told them, "My father and I and the Old Man were on a hunt. We came to a stream, and the Old Man told my father to walk upstream a little, and to look at the bank, to see what kinds of tracks could be seen, what kind of animals had come for water. The Old Man then motioned for me to come with him, downstream a bit, to look at the bank there, "Quiet", the Old Man signed to me, "make no noise". As he spoke, Schut made those same signs with his hands.

"But as we stood near the edge of the water, we heard a *great* noise", Schut told them, everyone hanging on his words. "With a great crashing sound, rocks, sticks and leaves flying, a full-grown bull elk jumped from the bushes that were between the Old Man and where my father had walked. It seems that the elk had been sleeping in the thick brush, it also seems that the Old Man and I had been quieter than my father. When the elk realized that my father was quite close to him, he did not yet know that the Old Man was even closer, in the other direction."

"Rushing to escape my father, the great animal caught sight of the Old Man just as the elk broke out of the brush. The elk jumped up and clean over, as the Old Man fell, and tumbled and rolled, trying to get out of the way". The expressions on all the faces had changed from great sorrow, to open-mouthed surprise as they waited for Schut to finish the story. "The elk ran down the trail, sounding like a whole heard of animals. As the Old Man tried to sit up, looking like a storm had struck, dust and leaves all over him, my father also burst through the hole in the bushes, left by the great elk." Making a face that looked like his father's own surprised face, Schut continued "my father said '*There was an elk! In the bushes! Did you see him?!?!*' The Old Man looked at my father, with a face still full of shock, and said, very softly, 'yes'. As we looked around at each other, and came to understand what had happened, we all sat down in the dirt and laughed, until we could not breathe."

Laughter quickly replaced the sobbing sounds coming from the people. The Wolf smiled. Not only at the humor in the story, but because he knew the Old Man well, and knew that he enjoyed this kind of tale. He would have wanted the people to leave the fire with this uplifted feeling, and not one of fear, or sorrow. "Tomorrow," the Wolf said, in his booming voice, "the Cloud people will come and join the Rock people. Together, we will walk to the Place of Waiting. We will all see, that the Old Man comes to his place of rest". Quietly, the group stood, and headed to their lodges to sleep.

Ach smiled as helped Sana to her feet. Sinc did the same for Ayea. Both of the girls now had bellies that were growing full and round. In the mid-to-late summer, their babies would arrive. The idea of being a father had at first been exciting to Ach, but now, with the loss of the Old Man, he felt an added weight upon his shoulders. Not only would the village look to him for his support and leadership, but now these two new lives, his own child and the child of his cousin and close friend, Sinc, would depend on him as well.

- o 0 o -

Decisions

Out on the Flat, the four young Walking Men, the girl, and the baby boy sat, without food, without their families, as the sun set and the sky grew dark. "What will we _do_?." asked one of the boys, "where will we _go_?" "We have no food here," another continued, "and we cannot hunt the large animals alone, they will kill us." "Back down the plain!," the first shouted, "we can join one of the other groups, the groups that pass the cold times near the place we do!"

The oldest of the boys was named "Zhe-Te", ghost. He was skilled at sneaking up on the large animals. He would watch them, and tell the other Walking Men which way the animals were moving. The hunters trusted him, and would take up positions where he recommended. He had hunted many times, but never alone. The large animals often needed several spears before they would go down. During this time, the wounded animals were very, very dangerous.

"No," Zhe-Te said. "The other Walking Men winter near us, but they are not _one_ with us. They are different, and maybe dangerous, especially to the girl", he counseled. "You do not _know_!, You are not _White Hair_!, We do not follow _you_!", said the youngest boy, with fear driving the tone of his voice. The breeze had died down and the silence of the plain was strange, here, in the middle of what had once been the Walking Men's camp. "Yes," the final one said, "back down the plain."

One of the girls that had gone to the Rock village was Zhe-Te's sister. For him, the choice was clear. "The Rock Men said we would be welcome," he said to the group, "My sister is there." "My sister is here," said the youngest, in a faint voice, "somewhere." The second oldest of the boys was "A-jee", tall grass. He too was a skilled hunter, but he also knew that a "tribe" of four boys, a baby and a wounded girl was no match for a herd of the large animals.

"Yes," he said, "I say we go to the Rock Village." The stars shown brightly above them on the flat, empty plain, as they tried to find a place to lay down for the night.

As the sun rose, decisions had been made. Two pairs of tracks lead off, back down the plain, made by the two younger boys, before dawn. "We will not see them again," said Zhe-Te. "They took the last of our food," said A-jee, "what will we eat now?" "Then we must go, and quickly, for the baby will be hungry too," Zhe-Te said. They looked around and found a skin that could be cut, to make a pack to carry the baby. Since the girl could not use her broken arm, they fixed the baby on her back. The boys found a couple more skins, a spear or two, and a bag for water.

Their hearts were heavy as they left their families there on the Flat. The sky was again filled with the birds that eat death, but they could not think of that now. They needed to walk, as quickly as they could, so they could reach other people, and food. They tied up the girl's arm, to support it. She said she could walk, so they began. Tracing their own tracks in the mud, they headed toward the mountains, toward food, and friends, and safety.

Sleeping once more on the edge of the Flat, they continued along their trail, until they reached the Lake village, as darkness approached. The Lake men recognized them, having seen them only a few days before. From the tear-stained cheeks of the young Walking Men, the Lake Men knew that something terrible had happened, though their words were too different to understand. The Old Woman of the Lake village called to the girl, and looked at her arm. She called to a Lake woman who also had a small child, and motioned for her to feed the baby boy. As the young Lake woman took the hungry baby to her breast, the Old Woman worked on the girl's arm.

The boys were able to sign to the Lake Men that they were traveling to the Rock village. The Lake Men gave them food for the trail, and another bag to carry water. Then, two young Lake Men signed that they would walk with the young Walking Men, to help carry their load, and to carry the baby. The Old Woman gave the girl a piece of dried fish. She showed her how to chew it for the baby, to spit out the bones carefully, and place small bits in the baby's mouth. She signed how much to give the baby, and that it would last about 3 days, enough to reach the Rock village. She signed to give the baby water, and to wrap him, and keep him warm.

As dawn came, the group signed "thank you" to all the village men and women, and again they started to walk. They were comforted by the company of the two young Lake Men. Their words were too different to talk much, but they felt much better, now that they were not alone. The girl was able to walk easier, now that her very young body didn't have to carry the weight of the baby boy. They made a good pace as they walked, back up river, trying to remember which valley stream lead up to the Rock village.

-o 0 o-

Water

Cree made a point of keeping herself busy. Her hands were always moving. Before the cold times, she had gathered sticks and several other items to work on during the many days when it would be too cold to go outside. She had some finely ground material of different colors that she could mix with water or fat to make paints. She would break sticks into short pieces and rub them on flat stones to shape them. She would poke a hole through these pieces with the holing tool Sinc had made for her, to make beads that she could color, then string onto necklaces, for trading.

This winter, she remembered something that she had seen in her home village. She took a few sticks that were straight, but a little shorter than normal arrows. Instead of making arrow points for them, she just sharpened a point onto one end, and then carved a notch on the other end, to fit a bowstring. These she presented to Ach and Sinc, for fishing. The boys thought they were perfect. Poking through a fish was much easier than through the hide of an animal, so they didn't need a stone point, and shooting into water, there was no need to put feathers on the arrow. Since they didn't take long to make, it was no problem if the arrows were lost in the water. The boys had been eager to try them as the weather warmed up.

As Ach and Sinc looked quietly into the water for fish, they noticed something was different. The stream was usuallyv rushing quite fast during the early part of the warm time, as the white cover up in the mountains quickly melted. But now, when it should be rushing, it looked slow and lazy, the way it usually did in late summer, when less water flowed into it. Ach remembered talking with the Old Man, who had mentioned that the snowfall during the cold time had been less than other years.   Light snows made for easier walking in the high country, but it had concerned the Old Man.

Ach also remembered that the rains had been light and infrequent during the last summer. Light rains and light snows had combined to reduce the water available in the stream. He wondered what it would look like if the dryness continued to mid-summer. This stream was very important to the Rock village. It was the only near-by source of water to drink. The Cloud village, well upstream, at the high end of the valley, had a small spring near their village. It was not big, but at least it produced enough water each day for the Cloud village to drink. But for the Rock village, if the stream went dry, the people would be in trouble.

But the thought that now stirred fear in Ach's stomach, was not of water, but of fire. From the valley floor, he looked well up on the ridge and saw several old, healing, burn areas. The burned trunks of trees, their limbs and leaves all gone, looked like straight, black spears sticking up through the recovering brush. The animals loved the area because the new growth of brush and grass gave them much more to eat than the thick, tall trees had done. This meant hunting was good along the edges of the burn, and the men climbed up there often.

It wasn't the difference from old forest to new brush that worried Ach. What he feared was the violence of that change. He feared the way the fire consumed all in its path. The fires, high up on the valley wall, were usually caused when storms brought lightning. The combination of dry brush, high winds and the spark of lightning often ignited the forest. But usually, since these fires began on the leading edge of a storm, the rains that came behind the storm would cool and dampen them, limiting the damage. Ach now worried about how dry the valley floor seemed, how easily the dust kicked up, how much brush there was to burn. Trees were not the only thing that might burn. If the village houses were damaged, winter could be very difficult.

98

-o0o-

Watching

It had happened several times lately. As Ach, or Sana, had risen early, and walked down to the stream for water, they saw Ash-Ká, sitting on a rock, watching the path that lead up the valley, from the river. She had awakened, well before dawn, and could not sleep. She worried about her mother and her father. As the weather had warmed, the mother of Ash-Ká had asked to visit her home village. Since the time Ash-Ká's parents had married, her mother had not seen her own parents. This was common for young women. Life could be hard, and travel could be dangerous, and both the man and the wife had constant work to do in their own village.

But Ash-Ká's mother was a good woman, and a good wife. Times had been pretty good since the weather had begun to warm up, and so Ash-Ká's father had spoken to the Old Man. The home village of Ash-Ká's mother was not so far. A day's walk down the valley to the river, and then two days walk up river. The Old Man said there was not too much work to be done then, in the early summer, and if the mother wanted to make the trip, the father should go with her. Ash-Ká was rather small for such a walk, and so her father had left her in the care of Ach and Sana. The father expected that they should return in about two hands of days.

But now, more than four hands of days had passed since they left, and there was no sign of her parents. Ash-Ká kept a close eye on the path. Each time she saw someone walking up the valley, she ran to see who it was. Several times now, she had been disappointed only to meet Rock men or Cloud men returning from a hunt, or the village women returning from a day's foraging.   With each new day, Ash-Ká's worry grew. She was not sleeping or eating well, and Sana worried about her.

This time, when Ash-Ká saw people on the valley trail, it was the sad remainder of the Walking Men, just two "Walking Boys", a girl and a baby. The Lake Men followed them, slowly up the valley, on the trail that followed the stream. Ash-Ká ran to meet them, only to be disappointed again. In tears, she ran back to the Rock village. Ach and Sinc saw this and hurried down the valley to meet the boys. Tears again stained the cheeks of the two boys and the girl, as they tried to sign what had happened. Their signing was difficult for Ach and Sinc to follow, until the boys gave the sign for "gone". All. It was clear.

Ach and Sinc helped with the things the boys were carrying, as they walked up to the village. They would feed the boys, the girl, the baby and the Lake Men, and try to find out more about what had happened. Before long, it was clear, this small band, all that was left of the Walking Men, would now need to stay with the Rock village.

The Rock people came together and welcomed the new arrivals. They listened as Ach explained what he thought had happened. One of the Rock women with a baby signed for the girl and the baby to come with her. She had room in her lodge, and she would ask her husband to take the two in. Since the Old Man's lodge was now empty, and since the two young Walking Men were certainly not children, Schut bedded them down in there. It was the first time in their lives they had slept in, or had entered, a permanent lodge. As first light came the next morning, the Rock women gave the Lake Men some dried meat and berries. The boys and the girl thanked them as the Lake Men headed off, back toward home.

-o0o-

Move, or Wait?

Ach and Sinc wanted to talk with Schut and Schut-Tah, about the water in the stream. "Father", Sinc said to Schut-Tah, "we are worried about the amount of water." "Why?", asked Schut-Tah, "it is low, but it still flows, there is water to drink." "Yes," said Schut, "it has been low before, but in my time, I do not remember it stopping." "Before the Old Man died, I heard him talk about the snow, and how it was not deep", Schut continued, "but he did not say the stream would go dry."

It had become normal for Ach and Sinc to be involved in discussions about hunting, and about the safety of the village, but now they found themselves in a difficult position. They *feared* that the stream would stop, although no one now alive had ever seen it so. They *feared* fire, but fire had never damaged the village before. They had fears, but their voices were not the lead voices in the village…that had always been the Old Man. He spoke, and the others listened.

Now, Ach and Sinc had to find a way. They had to make a plan, and get the people to listen. They decided to speak softly about their concerns, for the moment, and to continue to watch the stream. They would place some sticks in the stream, sticking in the mud, with marks on them, so they could see if the water got lower. As they neared mid-summer, it was clear, the water was still going down. The boys decided to bring the issue up at the council fire, at the full moon.

Just before the moon, Ach and Sinc saw the Wolf on the trail. They asked if they might speak with him, and since he liked and respected the boys, he found a place in the shade and they all sat down. They spoke of the dryness in the valley, the dust, and the dry brush, and they spoke about the water. "What do think you should do?", asked the Wolf. "Move," as these words left Ach's mouth, Sinc cringed, for he feared that the Wolf would laugh at them. "To where?" the Wolf asked, not sure he understood what the boys had in mind.

"We should make a camp at the end of the valley," Ach said with confidence. "If the stream runs dry, we will be close enough to the river to get water there. If fire comes to the valley, the people should be safe there. We can always repair damage to the lodges, but getting caught by a fire could kill the Rock people." It was clear that the boys were quite concerned, and it was clear they had been thinking long and hard about this problem. The Wolf rose to his feet, "If you feel strongly about this, then we must speak of it, at the fire." This is what the boys wanted. They wanted to know that if they stood up at the fire, they would not be alone.

At the full moon, the two villages gathered at the Council Fire as they always did. There were many small things to discuss, and the people always like having the two villages together, to have a chance to talk, and trade, and catch up. When it seemed like the proper time, Ach and Sinc stood to speak. To their surprise, the Wolf stood and, with his booming voice, asked the people to be silent, and to hear the boys. "They are worried about something," he said.

Ach began to describe what he and Sinc had been thinking of for at least two moons. He spoke of the light snowfall. He spoke of the light rainfall last summer. He spoke of the dryness in the valley this summer. He spoke of the sticks in the stream, and the falling level of the water. He spoke of the danger of fire, and what might happen if one raced through the valley. With Sinc standing beside him, he came to his conclusion: "the Rock people should move to a summer-camp at the end of the valley, near the river, soon, before the stream runs fully dry."

The Rock village looked at the boys in silence. Moving the village, even temporarily, seemed like such a drastic step, even a little crazy. Would the stream really run dry? If so, why not wait until it did, and then move? Schut, Schut-Tah and the other men didn't know what to think. To the others, who had not heard of this from the boys before, it just seemed like too much. It was too difficult to believe. Ach and Sinc were respected by the people, but even still, some felt themselves ready to laugh at the idea. Ach was afraid that the people would not listen. This moment, in front of the council fire, where such decisions should be made, might be lost. And just then, The Wolf stood up again.

"Ach," he said in his confident voice, "you spent much time with the Old Man, you listened well to his lessons. If he were here with us tonight, what do you think _he_ would say?" Confidence filled Ach's heart, this was just what he needed. Ach said, "I spoke with the Old Man of many things. One thing is clear in my mind," he continued, "When we would have some decision to make, the Old Man would say 'we can decide, or we can wait, until time decides for us'. He explained that sometimes, letting time pass may mean that some of our choices are no longer possible. That is what he meant by 'letting time decide for us'. But, the Old Man said that 'if a decision is made _for_ us, we may not like it'." The crowd was silent, their doubt was reduced a bit, but not removed. "We should decide now. If we do not, time may limit what we can choose." Ach turned to Schut and to Schut-Tah, and again recommended that the Rock people move. "Let us think about it, and talk about it further", Schut suggested.

As the people walked back to the Rock village, with Ach and Sinc still wondering if the village would agree with them, Zhe-Te and A-jee, the young Walking Men, came to them. "If the people move, A-jee and I can help," Zhe-Te signed and spoke, "Moving is our _life_. We can build lodges of skins, we can show the Rock people how to move a village. A-jee and I will help!" "Yes," Ach said, "there will be work enough for all. Let us begin tomorrow, to look at the village, to think about what we must take, and how we can carry it."

-o0o-

Planning

When morning came, the Rock men began to discuss in detail what they might do. Of course, there were many questions: "If we move, can we hunt in the same areas?"…"What about 'Outsiders', walking along the river trail…what if they are unfriendly?" "What if there are Coyotes?"…"If we were on a short trip, we would sleep out under the sky, but with the women and children, and if we stay for some time, we will need lodges…How will we build them?"…"If fire comes to the Rock village, how can we prepare for it?"…"We have gathered some food for the cold times already, should we take it, or hide it, as we do when raiders come? In the small caves, the food should be protected from fire, but how do we decide when will we return to the Rock village?"…"What will the Cloud people do?"

There were these questions, and many others. Ach could hear right away that some of the men could see the danger, but others, while not openly challenging the decision, were still not confident in the plan. Some of the questions showed interest, and showed participation in the decision, but others still indicated large doubts that the idea was a good one. The Old Man had always believed that the best decisions were the ones that did not seem to come from a single person, but from the group. When decisions were made like that, they were decisions that held firm, they were plans that did not fall apart. But Ach still worried about this one.

So, one by one, they discussed their questions, turning them over and over, until most of the people were satisfied. "If we walk a half-day down-stream now to hunt, then it is not so different to camp near the river, and walk up-stream a half-day. So, we should be able to hunt the same ground," one of the men concluded. "If we are worried about people who walk along the river trail, then maybe we should make our camp up-stream from the river a little. There is a clearing there which would not be seen from the river trail," another said, "and like always, we will watch for strangers. We should be ok there."

Zhe-Te asked if he could speak about shelters. Ach and the others were interested and drew near to him. Zhe-Te was surprised, and felt it quite a compliment that the men would listen to such a young boy, and one who had been a member of the village for such a short time. "A-jee, hold this," he instructed, and A-jee stood to hold two spear-length poles, tied together near the top ends. A-jee spread the bottom ends apart as Zhe-Te lifted a second pair of such poles, and did the same. Zhe-Te then placed a similar pole across the tops of these.

He tied the ends of this top pole to the tops of the others, and the poles stood together like a frame. Over this they lifted, with the help of a couple of the men, one of the large animal skins the Rock men had received from the Walking Men. They pulled the edges of the skin outward, making room for several to sleep underneath. The men looked at it, as Zhe-Te signed that one could also be made with two elk skins. Then suddenly, Zhe-Te threw the skin off, laid the poles together at the end of the skin, and rolled them all up together. He and A-jee then lifted this roll to their shoulders, and smiled. They were ready to move.

The men seemed to be feeling that this move would not be so difficult after all. They decided to take skins with them that would be needed for the shelters and for sleeping, and to leave others behind in the small caves used for hiding food. They would take some of the stored food with them, but would leave other food in the caves with the skins, so, as the Old Man had told them, "if some were lost, all would not be lost".

The men then moved the firewood that had been piled near the village further away, so that if it burned, it would not damage the lodges. Since the walls of the lodges were made of rocks and mud, not much damage would be done, except for the stick-and-mud roofs. If fire did damage the roofs, some skins could be thrown over the top for a quick repair. As preparations were made, Ach and Sinc were pleased. The village was working together, thinking together, deciding together.

But not all were "*together*". At least four of the men seemed to hang back, not participating in the discussions. They saw that the lodges were made of stones, and so they thought that they would be safe if fire came, ...*if* it came, and they doubted that it would.

As all seemed ready, the group gathered again to talk. It seemed that most of the group's concerns had been addressed. It seemed that the people were ready to move, and that most felt that the idea was right. Ach said that the end of summer should bring the rains that came with the cooler weather. When those rains started, it would be a good time to return to the village. Until then, the people should continue their usual hunting, gathering and preparing for the cold times, as they did every summer, but this time, from their temporary camp.

-o0o-

Moving Day

The night before the big day, before they lay down to sleep, Zhe-Te told A-jee to drink water. "I want us to wake early, I want us to be everywhere, helping everyone with this move," Zhe-Te said. A-jee understood. Like the girls who came to the tribe as new wives, the boys wanted to be seen as helpful, as useful, even necessary, to the village. They wanted to fit in. It was kind of the Rock people to take them in, and they wanted the Rock people to continue feeling that taking them in was wise. "And the water?" asked A-jee. "The water will wake us early, to pee. White Hair taught me," Zhe-Te replied.

It worked, and the boys woke in time to wake Ach and Sinc, and tell them "first-light" was coming. Of course, Ach and Sinc were pleased at this show of initiative, but they already knew that the boys would be a value to the village. The boys had worried that their skill at hunting the large animals on the Flat would be of little use to mountain people like the Rocks. But Ach and Sinc had seen that the boys were everywhere, helping prepare for the move. Almost everyone asked their advice, and this pleased the boys greatly. In time, the boys would learn mountain hunting, even teaching new hunting skills to the Rock men.

The move did not have the precision that would have accompanied a move of the Walking Men's village, because the Rocks had never done this before. But the boys were indeed everywhere, and with their help, the Rocks packed up everything they way they had planned, and laid out the loads that would be carried. The women had already moved the skins and food that would be hidden and left behind, so now the only items left in the village were the ones that would go to the summer camp. A bit sluggishly, but with purpose and intent, the Rock village began to move.

Well, *almost* all of the village. Standing near the trail was a small group of men. Ach went over to speak with them. "Ach," one said, politely, but firmly, "we will stay here." "We will be fine here," said another, "our wives and children will stay with us, we will continue to hunt, and dry meat." "If fire *does* come," another said, "we will shelter in the lodges. If the water *does* stop, we will join you at the summer camp." Ach was convinced that moving was best, but he was not fully convinced that staying would lead to certain tragedy. He knew that he should not try to force the men, or argue. He smiled, touched the men on their shoulders one by one, and said he would see them again soon.

Ach then noticed that he did not see Ash-Ká. He wasn't worried, because so many mornings lately, he had found her at the stream, watching the path that comes up from the river, watching for her parents. He saw Sana returning from the stream and asked if she had seen Ash-Ká, but she had not. "Look in the lodge", Sana said. There, snuggled down into the lodge skins, he found Ash-Ká, sleeping peacefully. Given her recent nervousness and constant watching for her parents, Ach was puzzled. He reached down and tickled her foot to wake her, she smiled. This smile puzzled Ach even more.

"Ash-Ká!", he said, "I'm glad to see you sleeping, but we need to be up, we need to be moving." She smiled again, a smile he had not seen since she began to worry about her missing parents. "I thought I would find you by the stream, watching," he said. "No, it's ok now," Ash-Ká said. "It is?" Ach asked. "Yes, she told me they would meet us at the new camp," Ash-Ká replied. "She?" Ach asked, puzzled. "Yes", Ash-Ká said, "the lady." "What lady?" Ach asked. "I had not seen her before, but she knew my name. She said 'do not worry Ash-Ká, your mother and father will find you at the new camp' ", Ash-Ká explained.

"What did this lady look like? " Ach asked. "Hmmm…well, she looked 'different'," Ash-Ká said, "not like the other Rock or Cloud women." "This is strange", Ach said, "when the Old Man died, I saw him, standing on the hill, with a woman, a woman who looked, well, 'different'. He had told me once, that sometimes, when he needed confidence, needed guidance, he would see a woman. He called her, 'the Spirit Woman' ". "Hmmm," Ash-Ká wondered, "maybe you and I will see her now?", as she snuggled back down into the warm skins. "Maybe," Ach said, "but you better jump before Sana comes and shakes you out of there!"

- o 0 o -

The River Camp

At the end of a long day's walk, the Rock people began to arrive at the site of the summer camp. The women sent the boys off looking for firewood before darkness fell. The children scampered about, but their mothers told them to stay close, until the women could have a look at the area in the morning light, to look for places that snakes might hide, or where children might be tempted to fall into the river. The two young Walking Men asked Ach and Sinc where the shelters should be placed, and began setting them up. Much more quickly than the Rock people had expected, their new camp started to look well planned and organized.

Ash-Ká found a stone by the stream where she could sit and wait for her parents, but now, her fear was gone. She was quite sure they would return, safe and sound, and she thought it would be soon. The group would eat more fish here, as there were more fish in the river than in the smaller stream, Cree thought about that and thought of making more "fishing arrows".

All day, as they had walked, Ach noticed the wind. There was always wind in the valley, sometimes a light breeze, sometimes gusty winds with storms, but this seemed different. Now, each time it blew, Ach thought about the dryness, thought about fire. If fire started, it would be the wind that would spread it.

Close to the end of the third day, as night was nearing, Ash-Ká came running into the camp. "Ach!...Ach!...They are coming!" she yelled. Ach followed her back to the river path and looked. Indeed, four people were walking along the trail. There was a man, looking weak, being helped by a woman, and two other men. Ash-Ká hurried down the path, and Ach hurried after her.

Momma!" Ash-Ká called, "Pappa!" Ash-Ká ran ahead, and Ach, not sure who the two other men might be, ran after her. One of the men stepped toward Ash-Ká. He went down on one knee and held out his arms. She stopped well out in front of him, not knowing him, but thinking that he looked familiar. "You are Ash-Ká?" he asked. His hair was combed and braided. He wore several necklaces around his neck, and the staff he carried had many marks. Ash-Ká nodded. "I am Na-Hé-ne…I…am your *Grand Father*", he said in a warm voice that Ash-Ká found friendly and welcoming.

The other man introduced himself as Ash-Ká's uncle, younger brother of her mother, but not before Ash-Ká buried her face in the skins of her mother, and gave a great hug to her father. It seems that Ash-Ká's mom and dad had traveled to the village of the mom's family, as they had planned. But on the way, Ash-Ká's father began to feel badly, to grow sick, and weak. He had arrived at the village in such a state that his mother-in-law knew immediately that his condition was dangerous, and so she began to care for him.

They had intended to stay for only a few days, to allow Ash-Ká's mother to visit with her parents, but had needed to stay until Ash-Ká's father was healthy enough to make the long walk back to the Rock village. As tired as he was, he was glad to see that the Rocks were now camped at the bottom end of the valley, saving him another long day of walking.

Ach greeted the Grand-Father and the Uncle, and invited them to the village camp. As they rested and ate, Ach signed and explained why the Rocks were now camped here, and pointed way up the valley to the Great Rock Wall, to show them the location of the village. The Grand-Father was a leader in his village as well. He listened carefully to Ach's concerns about the water, and about fire. He agreed with the decision to move the village, and liked the logic of moving when a choice was available, instead of waiting until they were forced to do so. He expressed his concern for the people who had stayed behind in the Rock village.

The next morning, as the Grand-Father and the Uncle made ready to return to their village, the sky was gray. Ach looked at the clouds and thought they would bring storms, later, in the warm part of the afternoon. He wondered about three of the men who had left the summer camp the morning before, to hunt up in the valley. He hoped they had their eyes on the sky.

Ach exchanged greetings of respect again with the Grand-Father and the Uncle, and invited them, if ever they wished to visit, to come and stay in the Rock village. The Grand-Father thanked him, and offered as well, to have the Rocks visit the village of Ash-Ká's mother.

The Grand-Father grinned, and pointed to the two young Walking Men. "We have some young girls in the village," he said loudly, "bring those two when they are ready to take wives." The whole group turned to look at the two young Walking Men, as their grinning faces grew red. As the two men walked back up-river along the trail, Ach again looked at the sky, and wondered.

- o 0 o -

Red Snow

Many afternoons brought high winds, blowing in from The Flat. These winds however, did not bring rain. The Flat was dry, and so the winds were dry, and the wind only served to further dry the trees and brush in the valley. One afternoon, as the wind rushed up the valley, Ach heard the beginning of thunder. The lightning was high up the valley walls, and so it was hard to see in the daylight, but the thunder was there. Over and over, it cracked and rolled down toward the river.

Looking up the valley, Ach could see people walking, down toward the camp, on the trail. He thought he could make out two women, carrying children. He and Sinc rushed up the trail to meet them, since it looked like they were quite tired. It was two of the Rock village women, who had stayed behind with the men. "We tried to get them to come'" one said, "but they laughed at us, for being afraid."

The women explained that on the day before, the lightning had been striking vey near the village, and that it was very frightening. They begged the men to lead the group to the summer camp, but they just laughed. "Ach has made you afraid," they said, "with all his talk of fire". "We were frightened, and when they laughed, it made us angry, so we picked up our children, and we left," the second woman said. "It took longer to walk, with the children. We walked most of last night, and all day today," said the first.

As the afternoon wore on, the light started to fade, and Ach was able to see the light from fires, up above the high trails. As the wind continued, gusting this way and that, the fire spread along the high ridges. Then, Ach saw something he hadn't seen before, high in the air, a mix of smoke and what looked like glimmering red snow. It was embers from the fires, blowing off the ridge, back out over the valley floor, softly settling into the dry brush. As the embers settled down, the light grew, as the sparks and wind combined to ignite the brush and dry leaves on the ground.

The wind still blew, gusting and blowing and pushing the fire across the valley floor. More and more of the valley was ablaze, as Ached watched more and more embers, "snowing" in from the high areas. The camp near the river looked safe. The wind was pushing the fire up the valley, away from the summer camp, toward the Rock village, and toward the Cloud people. As the people in the camp rushed to a higher place, where they could get a better view, they turned to see whole trees exploding into fire. The fire seemed to become a storm of its own, blowing, swirling, consuming the trees and the brush as fast as it could.

All wondered what would happen to the Rock village. All were very worried about the four men, the woman, and the two older daughters who were still there. Could people survive such a storm of fire? And what would become of the Clouds. Had they decided to move? When the Rocks had moved to their summer camp, they did not know what the Wolf was planning for the Clouds. They felt that the Clouds would always have water, because of the small spring by their village. But what about the fire? What would become of them?

Through the night, the wind continued, blowing, gusting, spinning its way up the valley. And with the wind, the fire continued. Smoke filled the air, and so there was little the Rock people could see, but now and then a brilliant ball of fire would rise, visible from far away, as it slashed and consumed another stand of trees. Well into the night, they sat on the high place and watched, eager to know what was happening. No rain in this storm, just wind and embers, smoke and fire, rushing, up each side of the valley, and running up the valley toward the Rock village, and the Clouds. Finally, as the night grew late, the wind began to let up.

The next morning, all was still. This smoke hung in layers, filling the valley completely. Ach could see that some of the valley had not burned. A good portion of the lower valley, nearest the summer camp, still seemed to be intact. Ach called to the young Walking Men. They took some water bags to the river, filled them, and began to walk with Ach and Sinc, up the valley trail, to see what they could see.

Traveling only a short distance, they came to a burned place, laying across the valley floor. They could see just beyond it, to another strip where the trees were still intact. How could the fire skip around like this? Why were some places burned, and others not? Ach didn't have the answers, but he had hope that the valley above them may not be totally burned. Maybe, the Rock village was spared? Maybe the Clouds? It would be some time before it was safe to walk further. Knowing for sure about the Clouds, and the people in the Rock village, would have to wait.

-o0o-

Return

In another moon or so, the winds changed direction and the rains came again. Even light rains were most appreciated, as any water was good, but heavy rains would only have washed much of the ash and bare soil into the stream, so less rain was better in the beginning. After several of these light rains, green shoots could be seen, even in the worst burn areas, as the grass and the plants below the soil began to spring back to life.

As the water in the stream began to flow clearly again, the Rocks began their move back to the Rock village. All this time, they had heard nothing from the people who had stayed behind in the village. Maybe for them, walking down the valley was as hard as it was for the people in the Summer Camp to walk up. On the long walk back, all the people thought, and worried, about what they might find.

Some of the lodges were not so badly damaged. Repairs could be made to the burned roofs relatively easily, and so the people from those lodges could get back into their homes right away. But others were more damaged by the fire, and in one, the people found something terrible. It seems that the storm of fire not only burned the trees, but blew some of them down as they burned.

Unfortunately, one of the large trees, that had always stood tall and helped protect the village from winds in the valley, had burned, had broken, and crashed down onto one of the houses. Worse, this was the house in which the men, the woman and the girls who stayed behind in the Rock village had taken shelter.

As the people walking up from the summer camp arrived, they saw crows sitting on the fallen walls of the house. The crows were not eating. Unusual for crows, they did not even call out. They were not disturbing the rest of the dead. They perched in silence, on the broken walls, looking first down at the dead, and then back at the approaching Rock people. They sat, in silence, until the people drew close, as if to say they had been watching, looking out for the ones that had died. They flew away as the people arrived, again in silence, and were gone.

There were none of the birds that eat death. The fire had taken too much, there was little remaining for animals to eat. The heat had left nothing but four skulls, and many spine bones. But why four? After the women and the children had left the village and joined the people at the summer camp, it left four men, one woman and two older daughters at the village. Where were the three others? What had happened to them? Had they escaped? Had they died somewhere else? Or had animals taken their bones? Perhaps the people would never know their fate.

The food and skins that had been hidden away had been undamaged by the fire, even though a bear had found some of the food before the fire had come. But in any case, with the food that had been gathered and prepared at the summer camp, and the rest that had been hidden away, the Rocks should have enough for the cold times. At least they would this time. This time they had all hands preparing food during the summer, but now had seven fewer mouths to feed. Next summer, they would have seven fewer sets of hands to gather food. Their risk when the cold would come, would be higher.

As soon as Ach and the other men had settled the people back in the Rock village, they set off for the Cloud village, to see what had become of them. They were pleased to see some of the Cloud boys on the trail. The boys ran to tell the Wolf of the Rock's approach and he rushed to greet them. Both groups were quite pleased to see each other.

It seems that the Wolf had indeed listened to the concerns of Ach and Sinc, about the danger of fire, and had been watching carefully. He also had the Clouds hide away some of their food, in case they had to move out of a fire's way. The village had not decided to move to a temporary camp, as the Rocks had done, but nevertheless remained ready, in case danger appeared.

On the day that Ach had observed the fire racing up the valley, as he watched from the river camp, the Wolf had also been watching, from the high trails above the Cloud village. He sent runners back to the Cloud village to warn them, and the people quickly moved up to the high ridge and over, into the next valley. They had hoped that a move like that would get them out of the fire's path. Apparently luck, and a favorable wind direction, had made it so. Their village was not badly damaged, and their food was safe, so the Clouds also had come through.

Like the Rocks, the Clouds had six of their men and boys off hunting when the fire had come. They had not been seen since. The Wolf believed that the fire had caught them, somewhere on the high trails. He worried that their bodies might never be found. To the Rocks and Clouds, having their dead remain missing was troubling. Such dead would not be able to sit with the others, at the Place of Waiting, until they crossed over. Their spirits might wander in the valley, without rest.

The Rock hunters that had been out when the fire had come, had been lucky. Or perhaps as the Old Man would say, they had been not lucky, but ready. When they saw the fire coming they were near a small pool that remained in the nearly dry stream. They lay down in the water and covered their faces with skins. They lay down as low as they could, trying to breath in the smoky air without uncovering their heads. The fire came, and passed over them. They were safe. It took them six or seven days to make it back to the Summer Camp. They arrived naked, hungry, covered with mud and ash, but they arrived.

Ach and Sinc then told The Wolf the good news, they were both new <u>fathers</u>! Sana and Ayea had both had their babies while staying at the summer camp. Two healthy boys, and both mothers were doing fine. Ach and Sinc were pleased and proud, and The Wolf could tell so by the way they stood, chests out, and shoulders back. The Wolf smiled proudly. As Ayea's father, he, Schut and Schut-Tah would now be _grand_-fathers. As this news was delivered, The Wolf too seemed to grow a bit taller, his chest a bit broader. He grabbed his son-in-law, Sinc, around the neck and wrestled in a laughing, friendly way.

The Wolf then said that the next full moon should be the last before the weather began to turn cold. "Now that you have returned, we must have a Council Fire," he said. This Council Fire would be a busy one, catching up on stories, introducing new babies, and speaking of the dead. Ach told The Wolf of the two young Walking Men that had now joined the Rock village, "We must welcome them, at the fire, before all the people," The Wolf replied.

One thing that seemed hard to find in the valley after the big fire, The Wolf said, "…is wood for making fires." He smiled, and joked, "though, after that, none of the Clouds have been too interested in building large fires." As Ach spoke to The Wolf, about walking to the un-burned areas to collect wood, Zhe-Te and A-jee looked at each other. They knew what their next way of showing their value to the Rock village would be.

And so life in the valley began to get back to normal. The men could hunt the un-burned areas, their walks were a bit farther, but there was game, and they were successful. The women would have to range farther from the village in the spring, when they started again to gather food. They would have to learn which kinds of food would be available in the recovering areas, and which they would have to search harder for, or just do without. But in time, all would recover.

The main lesson of the fires was that by planning ahead, and working together, disaster had been avoided. Most of the Rock and Cloud people had escaped the blaze. Both villages had enough food, and enough shelter to get their people through the coming cold time. As always of course, getting through the cold times was the main mission of all the Rock and Cloud people. The cold was a bitter enemy, and it took the efforts of all to defeat it.

-o 0 o-

Face to Face

As life in the village returned to normal, Ach decided to go off by himself, to hunt, to relax, and to think about the things that had happened. Walking alone, darkness was near. Down from the high trail and into the valley, but still far from the Rock village, Ach would find a place to sleep for the night.

The weather was warm and he had slept alone in the forest many times. He walked quietly, as a hunter should, always aware that food may be around the next turn. Wait, just there, some movement, low in the high grass, moving this way and that. A rabbit? Ach put arrow to bow, and crept forward. Rabbits like to stay near cover, they do not like the open, too many bad things can happen to them there.

Again, there it is. Moving toward that bush, maybe it will stop there and look around, look for danger. Ach raised his bow. The rabbit moved from the high grass, under the bush as Ach had expected, as he had hoped. Wheeew, the arrow flew, zip, it caught the rabbit. Food. Ach picked up the fine rabbit, a large one. He looked for a place to make a fire, a place to bed down for the night.

The fire crackled to life. The smoke was warm and pleasant. Ach cleaned the rabbit, opened it, and found some sticks to spread it wide apart. He found another, larger stick to hold it, out over the red coals. He liked rabbit. His mother cooked it for him often. When hunting large animals, the Rock people would eat some of the meat freshly cooked, but the rest they would cut into thin strips, to dry in the sun. This dried meat would last a long time. It would help them eat through the cold times. But rabbits and other small game were almost always cooked fresh, no drying. Fresh was better.

With the rabbit cooking, Ach scraped the skin and prepared to take it home with him. Rabbit skins are small, but the fur is soft and warm. Ach wondered what Sana would make from it, for his new son. When the rabbit was done, Ach began to eat. It was a large rabbit. He would eat well tonight, and have plenty for tomorrow. He spread out the deer skin that he would sleep on, and sat down on it to eat.

As he sat, the woods grew dark, and quiet, a warm and comfortable night. Then, as he ate, Ach noticed the shape of a face across the clearing, just outside the light of the fire, barely visible. Two pointed ears, and two black eyes. But the face was small, and not menacing. Neither Ach, nor the face, was afraid. He wondered how long the animal had been watching him. While he ate? Or while he cooked? Or maybe from the time he took the rabbit?

Ach took a bite of the meat, and then lowered his hand from his mouth, keeping still, keeping quiet. He watched the face as he put down the meat, but the eyes did not remain fixed to Ach's eyes…they remained fixed to the *rabbit*. "Ah," Ach thought, "this fellow wants a piece of my rabbit! Or, maybe, I am eating *his* rabbit." Since Ach had enough for himself, and more than enough for tomorrow. He flipped a small piece over toward the face.

To his surprise, the face did not spring forward. It glanced at the meat, and then back at Ach, then back at the meat. Finally, after watching for a long time, seeing that Ach did not threaten, the face moved. In a flash, it jumped out of the darkness, grabbed up the piece of meat, and disappeared. It was quick, but in the firelight,

Ach was just able to see, the face of a fox. Alone again in the quiet, Ach lay back and fell asleep.

In the middle of the night, an animal, maybe the size of a fox, ran, full speed, right passed Ach's nose as he slept. Jumping up, heart pounding, he threw some dry grass on the fire. Ach wondered what was running, or worse, what was it running _from_? "He-Na-Na-He!" he shouted, "He-Na-Na-He!" again. He lifted a heavy stone and threw it down hard, onto the ground. It made a sharp, loud, _"man-noise"_ that echoed across the valley.

"Shee-na-ne-teh, leh-a," a friendly, familiar voice came out of the darkness, "the mountain cat, has gone". It was the voice of the Old Man. "You remembered, to keep dry grass, to make light quickly," it said, "but you did not pee around your camp site." The pounding in Ach's chest vanished, he was alone, but in the company of an old friend. "The fox warned you," the voice continued, "now, pee on the rocks, and sleep". The mountain was silent again, except for a light breeze through the trees.

Ach chuckled to himself as he made his way around the camp site. As a boy, he always thought it was funny to pee on the rocks. The Old Man had taught him that the "walking hunters", the wolf, the fox, the bear and the mountain cat, would smell the ground as they made their way. When they smelled the pee of other animals on the rocks or trees, they would respect this "territory" and walk around if they could. He remembered the Old Man joking, "I only wish…it would work for snakes."

As Ach lay back down to sleep, he felt relaxed and comfortable. The air had been warm, but the wind had now changed, and a fresh new breeze blew down the valley. This kind of breeze signaled the turn of the weather, it would be cold again in no time. As he rested, the voice came out of the darkness again. "Ach," the Old Man's voice spoke, "the cold time comes…are you ready?"

It grew quiet again, but now Ach lay awake. He thought about the food that had been gathered, about the lodges that had been repaired, about the readiness of the people. He thought, and he felt restless. He had come away from the village to be alone for a while, but now he thought that his place was back with his people. At first light, he would make his way back down to them and make sure that all was done, that all were ready. The white cover would fall, and fall soon, testing them again.

-o 0 o-

Counting

Near the next moon, the village awoke one morning to the first white cover of the season. It was beautiful, as it always was, a soft white covering for everything in the valley. But as Cree looked at it, she could not help thinking of her mother, and how the harsh, white cold had taken her away. Cree did not celebrate the coming of winter, for her, it was a serious, fearful time.

At the end of the summer, the winds had changed and rain had begun again. The rain was generally light, but it was frequent. These light rains helped keep the runoff from the burned areas from choking the streams with ash and mud, and the frequency of them helped bring back the grass and bushes, making a bright green contrast to the otherwise blackened areas. But now, the frequent moisture meant frequent snow, and it began to pile up deeper than usual.

One of the old women in the Rock village had a string of beads. She and the Old Man had made it together. Her name was Red Bird, and the Old Man had appointed her *the counter of days*. It was easier for the Rocks and Clouds to note the Long Day in mid-summer. There was always plenty of sunshine at that time, so it was easy to see the position of the sun in the sky. In winter though, sometimes the clouds would hang heavy over the valley for several days at a time, sometimes giving no clue as to the height of the sun. So, instead of trying to observe the Long Night, they counted the days, with beads.

There were two hands of beads on a wrist-sized circle of leather. One bead was black, and the others light colored. This shorter loop of string was tied to the end of a long, straight string with three hands and three dark beads, plus two light colored ones. She would start her count on the short loop when the village confirmed the Long Day at mid-summer, counting a bead for each day. Each time she turned the full two hands of beads on the short string, she would move a knot on the long string over one more of the dark beads, day by day, slowly advancing the knot from one end of the long string to the other. When she reached the end of the dark beads, she then counted two more days with the little white beads, and announced that mid-winter had come.

Venturing outside in the cold and snow could be dangerous. But sitting in their lodges, eating the dried food and hoping for it to be less stormy or less cold, could be a long and depressing wait. It was important for the people to know when the middle of that long, dark time had been reached, because only then could they turn their minds to springtime. The announcement of mid-winter was a welcome and eagerly awaited event. It didn't mean winter was over, but it did mean that it would be... eventually.

In a more practical way of course, all the families watched the string of beads and thought about the amount of food they had left, to determine if their supplies would last. This frequent discussion and checking of food helped determine when and if it would be necessary for the men to go out and hunt. It wasn't that hunting in winter was difficult, quite the contrary. Since the animals in the high places would move downward, into the valley to find food, they were more concentrated and easier for the men to locate. The problem was, it was dangerous to be out in the cold. Bad weather could strike quickly, catching the men far from the lodges.

One of the biggest dangers of course was the sliding rocks and white that would come crashing down the mountain slopes. Over time, several hunters had been lost this way. This year, the many snows, the heavy, deep white layers clinging to the steep slopes, were ready at any disturbance to let go, carrying rocks, breaking trees and killing everything in their path.

The men had once approached one of these areas just after a large slide. They saw crows eating from a nice moose that had been killed. That winter the village was hungry, but the Old Man told the hunters to "stop". The meat of the moose was tempting, but the danger of another slide was too great. "Better to let the crows have it," he said.

So, as she had for many seasons, Red Bird counted her beads. At the turn of mid-winter, she would begin the count again, another half-year of beads, ending a day or two before mid-summer. Then, as always, she would start anew, correcting for any miscounts or slipped knots that might have occurred.

This year however, Red Bird had something else on her mind each morning as she reached for her string. You see, Red Bird was getting older. Her teeth were missing, as the Old Man's had been. Eating enough to survive winter was getting more and more difficult for her.

There was another, more ominous thing on Red Bird's mind. As she grew older, she feared that she was able to do less and less each year, for the village. All the people worked, because all the people would need to eat. As had happened in the house of Cree and Crow Woman, watching young ones become pale from lack of food made people think. Several winters, Red Bird had made sure that she was eating less, so the young ones would have enough. The others didn't see this, but through the cold times Red Bird would sometimes grow quite weak. Only when the beads and the checking of the food made her know the little ones would have enough, would she begin to eat fully again.

This year, as winter approached, Red Bird took Ash-Ká aside. She said "Ash-Ká, I need to teach you something. I need to teach you, about the beads."

-o 0 o-

Darkness

Mid-winter arrived, but the snow took no notice. It continued, almost every day, deeper and deeper. Wolves were near, many of them. At first, the people heard their howls at night. They were not afraid because wolves rarely came close to the villages. But now, as the prey animals higher up had come down into the valley, the wolves were forced to follow them. Worse, two different groups of wolves, competing groups, had arrived.

The howling at night became louder, more frequent, and closer. If one of the packs succeeded in killing a deer or an elk, the other pack stood near, eying the prize. As temperatures dropped, and hunger rose in the bellies of the wolves, the pack's fear of each other faded. Now, the wolves could be heard, sometimes just outside the lodges, fighting over the fresh meat. Growling and biting, violent, loud noises filled the night. It frightened the children. It frightened the women. It frightened the men.

Ach and Sinc told the women to be very watchful, even in daylight, when they went to the stream for water. "Never," Ach instructed, "go alone." But they didn't have to be told. The fearful wolf sounds were so frequent, and so close, that the women were already most careful about venturing outside. They kept the little ones strictly to the center of the village and had the men watch, weapons in hand, any time children would move from one lodge to another.

Calm lay on only one face in the Rock village, that of Red Bird. She saw the eager faces, coming to her earlier and earlier each day, asking, as they had asked just the day before, "How many more" they begged, "how many days before the weather begins to warm…How many more?" They asked about days, but what they really wanted to know was "how many more _nights_". The stress of winter, the fear of the wolves and the wondering when it would start to warm again was taking its toll, but not on Red Bird. She had made her plan.

If she felt that the little ones in her lodge were growing hungry, if the men were not able to carry meat through the cadre of hungry wolves, Red Bird knew what she would do. She had now taught Ash-Ká how to count the days. She told her of the importance of it and of the different events during the year. The old lady knew Ash-Ká was bright, she knew the girl was close to Ach and that he would coach her if needed. Red Bird was calm because she knew she had passed on a skill so important to the people, and because she knew what would become of her.

There behind the lodges was a smooth, flat stone. It was out of sight of the lodges, but hopefully close enough that the wolves would leave her alone. If the time came, Red Bird would make her decision. She would wait until night, when all were asleep. She would take her lodge staff, a staff that had belonged to her man, dead now many seasons. She would tie the counting strings to the top of it, the way other lodges tied important items, and she would stand it against the lodge where Ash-Ká slept. The people would find the staff in the morning, and know that Red Bird was gone. They would follow her tracks, and find her sitting on the stone. Having left all her warm skins in her lodge for others to use, when they found her, she would be long gone.

One morning, as several of the women prepared themselves to go to the stream for water, Ash-Ká asked to go along. Warily, watching everywhere for the wolves, they walked, in a tight group, down toward the stream. As they neared the water, they noticed blood on the snow. There had been a terrible fight among the wolves the night before, in this direction from the village. If they could have put off getting water any longer, they would have, but now it was time. Suddenly, the women stopped short. From very near them, but exactly where they couldn't be sure, came a low, mean, growl.

"Backs together. Face out," Ash-Ká said, in a firm voice, "Where is it?" she asked. "Here, beside the trail," another woman said softly. There, hiding under a branch, nearly invisible in the heavy snow, lie a wolf. A wounded wolf, hurt in the savage fighting the night before. "Stand still," Ash-Ká instructed, "look him in the eyes." Ash-Ká, facing back toward the village, searched, hoping to see one of the men. There, just in sight, was A-Jee. Ash-Ká whistled, he didn't hear, so she tried again. Finally, he stopped walking and looked toward the group of women, who clearly looked like something was wrong.

"Point to the wolf," Ash-Ká said, again instructing. The three or four women facing toward the wolf, slowly raised their arms and pointed. A-Jee could not see what they were pointing at, but he knew he must get the other men and get down there. Quickly, he called to Schut and Schut-Tah. He signed for weapons, and pointed toward the stream. Schut called to another man and together they ran down the trail. Ash-Ká held the women firm, fearing that if they ran, the wolf would attack them. As the men arrived, Schut-Tah placed himself between the wolf and the women, as A-Jee's spear found the heart of the animal.

Red Bird kept counting her days. Finally, eleven hands of days after the long night, the sun broke through the clouds. Winter, as it always does, was ending. It wasn't yet spring, it wasn't yet warm, but the worst was over. Spring was coming and there was no stopping it now. Red Bird never reached the time when she felt she must act on her plan. "Not *this* winter." She thought, "not *this* time. Now, I will teach little Ash-Ká to watch the faces of the moon."

-o0o-

Photos

The Buffalo photo at **Business** is by my cousin, Connie Barr.

The Footprint photo at **Thunder** is by my father, Tom Laughlin.

The Bear photo at **The End** is by my friend, Andrew Adamcik.

All other photos, including the cover, are by the author, taken in New Mexico, California, and Finland.